John Daniels is a former language teacher and author with an interest in local heritage and history. He has lived for many years in the village of Lowick where the novel is set.

Research into language acquisition led to a PhD from Durham University. Current interests include writing and publishing on language learning and gorilla and rain forest conservation in South West Cameroon.

John is currently working on the sequel to *Isolde, Daughter of the Priest, The Journey to Rome, A Pilgrimage of Penance*.

Dedicated to Isolde, daughter of the priest, a fourteen year old girl from the community of Lowick, excommunicated in 1353.

From the very little we know of her from the excommunication document at Durham, two factors stand out that Isolde was the 'Daughter of the Priest'; when they were no longer supposed to be married, and her name Isolde. A strange name to give a girl from an impoverished rural community, one associated with the popular medieval legend of Tristan and Isolde, a tale of love and tragedy. A way perhaps to indicate by her mother or whoever named the child that this was a girl destined to lead a special life.

John Daniels

ISOLDE DAUGHTER OF THE PRIEST

A Story from Holy Island and Medieval Northumberland

AUSTIN MACAULEY PUBLISHERS™

LONDON • CAMBRIDGE • NEW YORK • SHARJAH

A CIP catalogue record for this title is available from the British Library.

ISBN 9781035811106 (Paperback)
ISBN 9781035811113 (ePub e-book)

www.austinmacauley.co.uk

First Published 2024
Austin Macauley Publishers Ltd®
1 Canada Square
Canary Wharf
London
E14 5AA

I would like to thank Annie my wife for her support and help in writing this novel and to Dr Michael Stansfield of Durham University Cathedral. Muniments for his advice on the excommunication document and life at the Holy Island Monastery and Lowick in the fourteenth century.

Part One
A Question of Miracles

Chapter One

The words came to her, out of nowhere, from all those years ago: 'Wait, wait here.'

Tristan said a man lying in pain, mortally wounded on the battlefield, waiting to die from his wounds or the sudden violence of a knife cutting his throat, had a moment when images from his life came rolling out before him. So, now, she thought back, to the very beginning of her tribulation leading here to this moment of terrible punishment; excommunication, the word resonating with the terrifying menace of damnation, the ceremony now of casting her out into darkness away from the comfort and light of the church.

She saw herself again as the small child, standing after evening mass by the door of the priory church on Holy Island, ignoring the instruction to wait to be taken over the causeway back safely home to her community, Lowyk. How as the others disappeared on their way home, leaving her on her own, she had walked on to try and join them, coming to the dangerous place the sea came to possess. Then, the moment in the dark as the waters came with the cries of devils all around and the sudden feeling of calm, the miracle of her survival, a small child of five defeating against all odds, the rising sea, and the forces of darkness. And so, her life had changed; she had become a person attributed with special powers, saved by Almighty God because she had His work to do but within the community isolated because Isolde, daughter of the priest was different.

She raised her bowed head and looked out into the dark space of the Galilee Chapel, lit for this service of excommunication by a single, flickering candle which cast little light, the soaring columns disappearing into the gloom above them. In front, two lines of monks like a military formation, hoods raised. Impossible to see their faces, Isolde wondered whether she knew any of them, brought from Holy Island to witness this awful ceremony. It was impossible to distinguish anyone, their appearance shadowy and insubstantial.

Complete silence, nobody moved, nobody spoke, there was a sense of foreboding, an unnatural stillness and anticipation, even the men beside her from her community, who had tried to show a lack of fear for the occasion, gazing around the chapel and making comments, whispering jokes, stopped shuffling, cowed now by the pervading sense of doom. Then the sound of a heavy door opening and of people approaching from behind them. A procession of clergy and monks moved into the chapel to position themselves by the large candle in front of them where Isolde now noticed a lectern had been placed.

A man in black with a gold cross around his neck, the prior of Durham, now came to the lectern, holding up the parchment in his hand, showing them the document; it was just possible to see the seal of the Bishop of Durham fixed to the bottom page; the document of excommunication that had brought them here.

The prior seemed to be waiting for something and turned around irritably towards the lines of monks behind him. A single monk now detached himself from the group and walked quickly to place himself beside the lectern. His failure to do so before, holding up this important ceremony and keeping the prior waiting was sanctioned with a few sharp words, the monk bowed his head.

A solemn voice now filled the silence as the prior slowly read the clipped Latin words from the document on which their sins were inscribed. Words Isolde could understand from her time at the monastery, the others, although Latin was familiar from Sunday Mass, would not understand. After each line of Latin embedded with certain elements of Norman French, there was a moment for the young monk to provide the translation.

He began his voice wavering:

'Inhabitants of Lowyk and parishioners of Holy Island.'

'Defendants who…took the corn tithes of Lowyk…of the months of August, September and October of 1351 and 1352 and…'

Here there was a longer hesitation and an awkward pause as a particularly difficult word was considered and then, found – "maliciously" the young monk repeated the word pleased, giving the word emphasis as the prior had done with the original Latin – yes, maliciously and he looked up at them pleased with the English word he had found threw them into pits for consumption by animals incurring excommunication.

He seemed to say the final word with emphasis, so it echoed around the chapel.

The act was seen as "malicious" an unacceptable and frightful action, only for Isolde and the others standing there representing an impoverished community on the threshold of starvation this had been a matter of survival.

The young monk now disappeared back into the row of monks, his work completed for now was the time to reveal those found guilty of what for the church was a heinous crime.

The name of each defendant was now read out, given prominence, pronounced with force and followed by a pause as though to ensure that the Almighty could register the names of the newly damned:

Gilbert Douff

Gilbert had stepped forward to stand a little way in front of them as they had formed, as instructed, a line. As reeve he was leader, responsible for the decision to keep the tithes for the community, to save lives in this time of famine and terrible hardship. He stood straight, looking ahead of him proud and unbowed, a man respected even though his decisions had led to them travelling all the way here, down the "Devil's Causeway", the old Roman road to Durham Cathedral for this declaration of excommunication:

Adam Brouse
John Day
Alan Patterson
Nicholas Forestor

20 names in all, almost all the men of the community. Only her father the priest and some old and infirm men had escaped proscription.

At the end of the list their names, the two women. There was a further pause. Was this, Isolde wondered to denote crimes going beyond the actual cause of the punishment? To include women and particularly a girl in the list in a world where actions were the responsibility of men was considered unusual, everyone said so. The fact perhaps that she was the daughter of the priest, when marriage was no longer an accepted position for someone in holy orders and for Marjorie, cohabiting, since her mother's death, out of wedlock, with the man, her father, who held this position.

There was more though wasn't there, she thought of the matter of her supposed special powers, her time, as a girl, learning in the monastery, the belief she had the ability to make miracles happen. And she wondered now, with increased fear, whether this sentence could be only the start of her humiliation. The word "witchcraft" came into her head, a punishment which went even beyond the terror of excommunication. Once removed from the church was it not, only a small step, to be seen as a heretic with the horrific punishment of burning at the stake.

She could see Brother William, now Prior of Lindisfarne, standing in the shadows, he seemed to be looking directly at her, the one who had brought these charges and would have specified the need to include the two women, to extirpate an evil which he saw as casting a shadow over the mission of the church of God on Lindisfarne, Holy Island. Would he go further to destroy her?

And she saw with foreboding that the Abbot reading from the list now stood aside as Prior William stepped forward to read the last two names. This was his triumph the ending of a particular endeavour to end the infamy of the special considerations with which she, Isolde had been endowed. He had reserved this final part of the ceremony for himself, he would pronounce their names, those responsible for blasphemy.

'And...' the familiar voice she associated with the threat of damnation, calling out now the final names on the list:

Marjorie Grubbe

'Finally.'

There was a further dramatic pause, which seemed to Isolde to stretch out into the furthest reaches of the darkness around them, beyond the solemn rows of hooded monks gathered to witness the ceremony:

'Isolde, daughter of the priest.'

Did she imagine the terrible power he put into the reading of her name, the way he emphasised "daughter of the priest", making it sound as though this in itself was an unforgivable sin.

There was no mistaking; he was now looking directly at her, a long moment, before slowly turning to walk away.

Her name seemed to resonate, hang in the air, as the ceremony came abruptly to an end: the Bible on the lectern was closed, the single candle extinguished, the hooded monks processed out of the chapel leaving them there alone in the dark, abandoned, as the single mourning bell tolled, signalling their death as members of the community of God.

Isolde couldn't breathe, a feeling of panic took hold of her, a terrifying sense of fear as though the punishment brought with it physical pain and suffering. Marjorie standing beside her caught her hand but she had to free herself and bent down, she was going to kneel but remembered communication with heaven was now forbidden.

Was this how she would die, collapse here in the dark, at this moment of agony as the excommunication was pronounced and the heavy door of the church with all its promise of light and hope, slammed shut in front of her?

Chapter Two

'Isolde, wait after the service here, at the church door do you understand, I will come and find you and take you home. But you wait here.'

He spoke slowly to make sure she understood.

'Promise, Mac?'

'Promise, I will come here and we will go together back home.'

She was quite clear what Mac had said, he would come here, by the priory church door to take her back across the sands where the sea came and then, up the hill to her village Lowyk a long, tiring journey for a small person. She asked her father, the priest, why they had to come all this way to mass here in the church on Holy Island and he had said how special it was, to be part of the monastery, one of the chapels on the island where St Cuthbert had lived, wasn't that something wonderful, she had nodded. But now waiting in the cold outside the church for her friend Mac, she didn't think it was such a good thing.

Mac Sout was always laughing and teasing her but he would carry her on his shoulders all the way down to the crossing point across the open sands back to her cottage next to the chapel. Only, he wasn't here now.

Isolde was one of the last to come out of the church and now looked for him among the crowd gathered outside, people from the other chapel villages: Tweedmouth, Ancroft, Kyloe and those she knew from her own. Prior Gilbert's sermon had gone on too long, people had been shifting about and muttering, and worried they would be unable to cross over to the mainland in time. Someone shouted out, 'We're going to get wet, Prior.' And people laughed, Prior Gilbert had paused in the sermon he was reading and looked up at them frowning.

Then someone else shouted, 'Don't stop, Prior!' And that had made everyone laugh again, a strange sound in God's church. And it was then that she and Mary had got the giggles, standing at the front of the nave so they could see. The prior carried on with his sermon a moment more, about how if you led a good life you went to paradise but he was now speaking more quickly and had brought the sermon to an end with a prayer wishing them a safe crossing and journey home but by this time people were already hurrying out of the church.

Mac, didn't come and soon all the people had gone past her, walking quickly to cross the sands before the tide cut them off, leaving them on the island. Mary with her mother had come out and asked Isolde whether she would come on with them but Isolde shook her head and said she would wait.

'Don't be long, Isie, you don't want to get stuck here with all those monks!'

And they had laughed, she didn't want to go to the monks but there was still no sign of Mac. She decided he would be waiting for her down at the crossing place, it would be his joke, making her think she had been left behind on the island, forgotten about. So, she started to walk quickly down the track from the village, along past the sand dunes. She had been alone like this before, a small figure under the open skies full of weird, wild sounds, the cry of birds, the howl of the cold November wind and the roar of the approaching sea, moving across the sands, flooding in to make Lindisfarne an island again.

She wasn't scared she told herself, even though it was getting dark and she was alone, just a little…a little worried. It took her some time to walk to the crossing place and when she got there no one was there, no sign of Mac or anyone.

She called out:

'Mac, I'm here, don't tease me please.'

But there was no answer.

She looked around her no one, nothing. She didn't know what to do; didn't want to go back to the monastery but looking across the sands in front of her, the way to cross, knowing the sea was coming but there didn't seem anything else to do, somebody would find she was missing and come to collect her wouldn't they. So she started walking down across the sand, still just able to make out in the dying light, the end of the path, where the land returned, it looked a long way.

For a few moments, she felt fine, brave, pleased with herself for doing this because this was the right thing to do, walking back because her father and Marjorie, who looked after her, would be worried. After a moment though, she began to feel anxious looking back over her shoulder at the way she had come, realising she was now away from the island, in a place where the sea could catch her, looking ahead, the dry land she needed to get to, had now disappeared into the darkness.

The wind was whistling around her making her feel cold, she put up her hood and as she did so, fearful images of monsters came to her, terrible winged and horned creatures sent by the devil to come for sinners. But they wouldn't come for her would they, she was a good girl, she told herself, did as she was told, everyone said how kind she was, a good person. Then she remembered giggling in church and the way the Prior had looked at them as he ended his final prayer. Perhaps she was going to be punished, she walked on more slowly, frightened, wanting to be home in front of the warm fire, out of the darkness, safe from evil, from the terrible things of the night.

It was then she realised with a shock her feet were getting wet, saw the tide racing in to come for her. She was soon surrounded by water, the safe sand had disappeared, and now she was standing in the sea. She knew the danger, had heard of people being drowned, everyone said it was because they had sinned, bad people punished by God.

And it seemed to her now that she could make out in the dark terrible shapes, creatures, she had seen painted on the church walls coming in with the tide to seize her, hearing on the wind their frightful chants, calling out her name over and over.

'Isssssolde, Issssolde, we've come to take you with us down into the cold dark sea.'

'IIssolde, you must be punissshed, drown for your sins.'

She screamed; she was only little, they couldn't do this to a child, shouting out to them, trying to make herself heard above the noise of the wind and rush of the sea.

'Five, I'm only five!' She held up her small hand in the dark night with her fingers outstretched, as she did when showing anyone how old she was, pleading for mercy.

But the voices continued their frightful screams and she started crying, looking at the sea, now all around her. She turned trying to work out where she had come from and where she had to go but everything was now caught up in the dark night and she no longer knew which way to go, setting out again she stopped afraid she was just heading out to sea.

Then, she remembered what she must do, she must pray, she must say the words, ask for protection, ask the Blessed Saint Cuthbert who had lived on this island, to save her from the rising waters, like in the story of Moses. He was a great saint; had special powers, he could part the waters, letting her walk safely across the sands to dry land, so she could go home.

Isolde forced herself to kneel in the cold sea which came up over her knees; pressing her hands together, closing tight her eyes, trying to shut out the darkness, the terrible presence of the sea around her and the howling wind with the cries of monsters.

'Blessed Cuthbert, come to me, come to me…' She could say the words only with difficulty. 'Help me, Isolde, your friend, make the sea go, let the waters part…like for Moses and let me walk home.'

She said this three times, it was all she could do to force herself to remain in the freezing water. Then she slowly stood up keeping her eyes tightly closed for a moment knowing what she wanted, wanting to believe in a miracle but afraid that things wouldn't have changed.

She opened her eyes slowly, there was no miracle, the sea had not parted, she could feel the energy of the waters rising around her and with the waters came a terrible fear, she was going to drown all alone in this horrible place, would never return home, see again her father, Marjorie, her dog Fortune.

Terrified, she thrashed about in the water, turning around desperately, looking about her for something that could help, shouting out for someone to come, that she didn't want to die, didn't want to drown.

After a moment, she became still again, stopped shouting, hung her head and waited, feeling the sea rising around her, giving up hope as the tears streamed down her face, there was nothing she could do.

Then, quite suddenly, something had changed, something was different. She looked around her feeling that she was no longer alone; someone was there with her in the dark, cold night. There was nothing she could see, she wasn't sure there were any words, just a feeling someone had come to help, to take her to safety.

It was as though she was being shown what she had to do, someone, something was now guiding her, making her turn back towards the island, helping her to fight her way through the water, it was difficult but the fear began to leave her for a feeling of calm, knowing she was going to be safe. The sound of the devils had gone; she just had to push on to safety through the sea, her movement parting the waters, forcing them back.

Once or twice she fell, being completely immersed in the freezing water but pulled herself up with difficulty, out of the clutch of the sea, shaking the water from her, shivering, but continuing to fight her way forward using all her remaining strength, before finally, the shore loomed up in front of her as she collapsed on the dry sand, safe, back on the island.

It was a moment before she came to her senses, to realise where she was and what had happed and then she looked out into the darkness where terrible things might have happened to her and shivered with cold and fear.

Remembering how her prayers had been answered, she knelt again, thanking Saint Cuthbert for coming to her help, before standing up and staggering back along the track towards the monastery. It took a long time because she was very tired, had to keep stopping to rest but finally, there was the shape of the monastery buildings in front of her and this time they didn't seem so frightening.

The big door to the church was slightly open and she walked inside, noticing for the first time the quiet beauty of the place, the tall columns and rounded arches which after the dark and cold seemed a place of peace and calm. She walked towards the altar, noticing in the dim light of a single candle the mural of Saint Cuthbert. She lay down on the bench in front of it and after a moment fell asleep.

News of the missing child had come shortly after the end of the service, as the community made their way up the hill towards their village and discovered Isolde wasn't with them. A frantic message was sent to the monks asking them to search the monastery and grounds to see if she could be found.

As soon as he heard this, Prior Gilbert began to fear the worst and when no sign of the girl was found in the monastery, he decided the child, separated from her family had drowned, caught by the rising tide. This wouldn't be the first time this had happened and he considered how blame would be attached to him for continuing his sermon when he knew that the tide would soon be turning. He had noticed two small girls at the front of the congregation and decided this Isolde, the one missing, daughter apparently of the priest, would be the girl with blonde hair, a pretty little thing with a big smile. He imagined the small, drowned body washed up on the sands and the difficult funeral, the anger which would be directed at God for allowing one of his children to die, and how his lengthy sermon had contributed to this death.

It was stupid of him, he knew he was going on too long but wanted in these terrible times to have his congregation realise, once more, that however hard things were in this life they should look forward to the life to come, the promise of paradise. At the funeral, he would of course provide them with the image of the girl in a better place, happy in the company of the blessed but knew this would not help the grieving community.

Gilbert went about his evening routine distraught by what had taken place, thinking constantly of the still figure lying alone at the edge of the sands; dreading the announcement which would come as soon as the girl was found at first light and brought here to lie in the priory church and then the arrival of the mourners, the wailing cries of grief as they came to the cold, lifeless body.

As soon as he could, he excused himself and retired to pray for the soul of the child, entering the church and sitting down on his chair by the altar. He looked around him at the magnificent stone pillars soaring up into the darkness, the special sanctity of the place heightened by the light of a single altar candle. It was a place he liked to come, to be on his own, thinking through the problems that came from his life as prior but tonight there was no comfort, only a terrible feeling of anguish. He dropped to his knees, closing his eyes.

He had come to pray for the soul of the child but found against all evidence that he was asking for her to be saved, that some miracle should have brought her safely from the trials of the sea and the terrible death by drowning.

'Lord' – and he paused wondering whether he could really ask for such a thing – 'Lord, I ask for your mercy as a humble sinner, one who deserves no blessing from you, that the child Isolde, might somehow have been saved from the waters.'

And then realising how useless this plea was, bowed himself to the fearful reality of death. 'And if as it must be she has died, I ask you for the soul of this small child, that she may come to you from her fear and death into the light, the warmth and comfort of your holy presence.'

He felt the tears on his cheek as he saw again how the girl had been standing in front of him in the church, saw her quite clearly and how now, she was lost forever.

'Lord, these are hard times but if in your mercy.'

He stopped aware of some movement in front of him and opened his eyes turning to see what was interrupting his prayers.

The girl was there, standing in front of him, completely still, no expression on her white face, her garments soaked, the figure he would expect, the vision he would expect from the drowned girl. But why had she come to him, what terrible message would she bring?

He looked at her for a long moment unsure how he should proceed, never previously having encountered a vision, not certain whether this would be someone you should talk to. And so, speaking slowly and carefully, afraid the thing would disappear before delivering the message he was sure she would bring, blaming him perhaps for her death.

'Who are you child?'

'I'm Isolde Prior Gilbert, daughter of the priest.'

He wanted to put out his hand to touch the figure, to prove that this was not the actual child but a vision but couldn't bring himself to do so.

'Why are you crying, Prior?'

And then he did it, slowly put out his hands and touched the child, felt the wet clothes, this was no vision, this was flesh and blood, she was alive and Gilbert was overcome with the feeling of the most complete joy he had ever known, in the midst of so much adversity here was something truly wonderful.

'You, you are alive, Isolde.'

There was the faintest of smiles.

'I'm very tired.' And with this, she collapsed onto the stone floor.

Gilbert picked up the small body, feeling the wet and realising she might not survive the experience, that she needed immediate attention. He carried her out of the church calling for help, for Brother Gregory who would know what to do.

'She's alive, the girl has been saved. Come quickly, she's very weak, she needs immediate help, food dry clothes, a hot fire.'

And the monks appeared from their business to look in amazement at this figure of their prior carrying the bundle of a small girl who everyone was sure had drowned and who looked as much, her head hanging apparently lifeless from the prior's arms.

And then there was Brother Gregory, who carefully took the girl from him, and nodded to say it was going to be alright that they would make sure she was made warm and dry and given the comfort she needed and Gilbert watched him carry this Isolde down through to the refectory where the women who worked in the monastery would help her.

He was still worried; wanting to be sure everything was in fact alright, pacing up and down the cloisters impervious to the cold, stopping to pray every few minutes.

Brother Gregory came back some half an hour later to report that the girl was strong and in good health and had been able to support her ordeal, had been given warm clothes and was now eating bread and honey with hot milk in front of the fire in the refectory.

'We must ring the church bells, Gregory, to tell the people of Lowyk that the girl is alive, they will be searching for her body on the sands, afraid to cross over at night for fear of devils, so they must be told.'

And then he walked to the refectory and there was the girl looking better, a little colour in her face now, wearing some monk's garment much too big for her with the sleeves rolled up.

Gilbert sat down opposite her, telling her she must continue eating to build up her strength after such a terrible ordeal.

'We were so worried about you but you are here now, safe and well, and he patted her arm wanting to be reminded again of her salvation.'

She nodded; her mouth full of bread and honey.

'I know you are tired but I will want to talk to you in the morning.'

'I'm staying here in the monastery?'

He nodded. 'With the ladies who help here.'

Gilbert paused a moment, so keen to ask further questions.

'I just wanted to know what happened, you started to walk across the sands and the sea came?'

She nodded.

'Then how did you survive?'

Isolde stopped eating and looked down at her small hands beside the bowl she was drinking from. She seemed unsure, perhaps slightly embarrassed and Gilbert knew he should wait until the morning, when she was refreshed to find this out. And stood up to go.

'I was very frightened, Prior. It was cold...the sea was rising, I was alone, surrounded...by sea.' She shivered, looking up at him to make him realise the awfulness of the moment. 'It seemed there were monsters, terrible monsters that wanted to take me then...'

'What happened, Isolde, this is important.'

There was a further pause.

'I felt that someone else was there with me, supporting me, that I wasn't alone any more, that, that it was going to be alright.'

Chapter Three

Prior Gilbert sat at his desk thinking about the problem he had. From what the girl had already said, it appeared that something very special and unusual had taken place to save her. He looked out of the window, it was a morning of bright sunshine, a morning of light after the grey of the previous days, the wind had died down; there was a feeling of peace and calm to match the delivery of this young child from the clutches of the sea.

His problem was, and he wasn't quite ready to pronounce the word yet, if there had been some kind of extraordinary circumstance which had delivered the girl, brought her to safety but he lacked the evidence he would need to make this official, an act of the Blessed Saint Cuthbert. He had only the girl's own account and he needed this morning, when she was brought to him, to question her carefully to find out exactly what had happened. She mentioned feeling she was no longer alone, that there was someone else beside her. Were words spoken, did Isolde actually see anything, a bright light and who actually did the girl feel had come to support her?

He didn't have much time, had asked for Isolde to be brought to him immediately after breakfast for he knew that at any moment her father the priest would arrive with others from the village, wanting to celebrate this salvation. He busied himself with preparing his quill pen ready to record exactly what she said had taken place.

The thing was that if she had been saved it wouldn't just be a merciful response, although it was obviously that. He considered the matter, putting down his pen and looking out again at the bright morning. Rather, it was that she had been preserved because she had been chosen for a reason, to do something special, carry out God's will in some way, ways that he would be unlikely to be able to fathom.

There was a knock and the door opened and there was the girl holding Susan's hand, the youngest of the kitchen helpers.

'Good morning Isolde, did you sleep well?'

'Yes, Prior Gilbert, very well thank you.'

'And she had a big breakfast, Prior, bacon 'n eggs, she ate all of it up, she's a big appetite.'

Susan left to go back to the kitchen. Gilbert made Isolde sit down on the stool in front of the desk, realising at this moment that he could do with a witness and shouted out after Susan to please find Brother Gregory and to get him to come. It was all taking so much time.

Isolde sat watching Gilbert dip his pen into the ink and write something on the parchment in front of him.

'Prior Gilbert?'

He looked up.

'Would you teach me to read and write, please?'

Gilbert smiled and was about to shake his head and explain how although lessons were given at the monastery, these were not available for girls. But then thought, if this had been, he paused and then said the word to himself a miracle, and this was a person specially chosen, then she should be

31

given all the education available, to make her stronger in the mission, the purpose for which she would, he supposed, have been chosen.

So, he said slowly that although usually learning to read and write was something available only to boys, boys of good families, in her case he was ready to make an exception.

'You see, Isolde, I think this is something you would find beneficial because...'He didn't finish the sentence, unsure what he could say, how he should express himself.

Brother Gregory arrived at this point and Gilbert began his questions.

'Now Isolde, I wanted to ask you some special questions about what happened to you last night, where you were, what you felt, what exactly you saw.'

She frowned, not apparently keen to talk about the experience.

There was a pause as the two monks watched her, waiting to see whether she was going to answer, Gilbert's pen poised to translate into Latin and then record her words on the parchment.

'It's difficult, I don't want to remember.'

'But wasn't it special?'

She put her head down and covered her face with her hands, as though wanting to shut out the memories, the fear. When she started speaking, she spoke very slowly without looking at them.

'I was alone in the sea and didn't know what to do, which way to go, there was no one to help and then I don't know what it was.' She shook her head.

'Did you see something, a light, or hear something, someone speaking to you.'

The child shook her head. 'I said my prayers to the Blessed Saint Cuthbert, knelt down in the cold water, and wanted him to part the water for me like Moses.' She looked up at them.

'And was he the one who came to help you?' This was Brother Gregory.

She was rocking forward on her stool, still looking down at her feet.

'But the sea didn't part, nothing changed.'

There was a pause and Gilbert was afraid she was going to say no more, or perhaps before she had time to say anything further, her father would arrive.

'You know when you have a good feeling.' She was looking up at them now, more animated. 'When things are going to be alright, that's what it felt like.'

'A feeling of calm?'

'Yes, a feeling that I shouldn't worry any more, someone was looking after me.'

There were the sounds of shouting coming from out in the courtyard and then the door of Gilbert's office was thrown open and there was Isolde's father, the priest and a small round woman in floods of tears, this would be Marjorie and a large dog, barking excitedly, which Prior Gilbert backed away from, he was scared of dogs, and then a tall, younger person who Isolde addressed first from out of the consuming embrace of Marjorie.

'Mac, where were you, you said to wait and you didn't, you didn't come!'

Chapter Four

Prior Gilbert looked at the man standing in front of him, the priest from Lowyk, Isolde's father; it appeared there was no surviving mother, another death in childbirth.

The man was standing head bowed, worried by this unexpected call to come and meet the prior and it wasn't clear how he would react to the request Gilbert had to make to him.

'I'm sorry to ask you to come here this morning but there are some things I wanted to talk to you about.'

The priest looked up, a worried looking man, untidy in appearance, not very old, perhaps 40 years but visibly someone who had suffered but hadn't they all suffered these last years.

'I wanted first to ask you about the corn tithes.' Better to begin with familiar territory.

The man's head dropped again.

'It's November and they still haven't been paid.' He waited for a reply.

The man sniffed and looked up at him again without saying anything.

He didn't need really to say anything they both knew the situation. The corn tithes hadn't been paid because there was hardly enough food to feed the community let alone find the additional corn for the monastery.

'You see, I'm worried that if no payment is received again this year we will be hearing from the bishop at Durham. I will be called to task and new measures will be put in place to ensure the tithe is collected and if this doesn't happen, I'm afraid there will be punishment.'

Gilbert looked down at his desk, this wasn't the way he wanted the conversation to go, it had been a mistake to begin with; the tithes a topic of huge controversy. The priest as everyone in the monastery's communities was caught in the middle of the argument between the village leaders and church authorities.

The priest suddenly became more voluble, speaking quickly, failing to hide his anger.

'I go to see the reeve and tell him what you the church are telling me and he says there is no way he can let his village starve, there will be no tithe paid this year, no tithe paid until there is enough food to ensure everyone has enough to eat. Then I come to you here on the island and you say that the tithe has to be paid.' He raised his arms. 'What am I supposed to do?'

Gilbert knew it wasn't worth going over the argument again, setting out the church position how if the tithes weren't paid by the different chapels the monastery would cease to exist, would have to close. There would no longer be a place for pilgrims to visit, no longer somewhere to ask for forgiveness, to be cured of an ailment at the shrine in memory to Saint Cuthbert – the actual tomb now and for centuries at Durham Cathedral but the whole reason for the building of the priory and setting up of the monastery had been to continue the worship of Saint Cuthbert here where he had lived and where he remained by far the most important saint to those who lived here, more important even than the Blessed Mary, mother of Jesus.

There was a pause as Gilbert considered how he should proceed on the more delicate matter concerning the priest's daughter, Isolde.

'I know things are difficult and this is something we should talk about another time. I wanted to talk about Isolde.'

The priest looked up suspiciously, the conversation now did concern him; this was his daughter, the dearest thing in his life, the child he had nearly lost forever.

'Look, it's Michael, isn't it, sit down, there's a stool by the door, you shouldn't be left standing there, can I get you a mug of water.'

The man shook his head and there was a pause as he brought over the stool and sat down in front of Gilbert's desk.

'What does the village say about what happened to her?'

'They say it was a miracle, all of them.'

'And what do you think?'

The priest looked directly at Gilbert and nodded his head.

'I think, yes, a miracle, a small child surviving the sea.'

'Unfortunately, we have no one else who can tell us what happened and so officially it doesn't count as a miracle.'

'Nothing else can be done to make it one?'

'I'm afraid not.'

For a moment, there was silence as they both remembered the incident of two days ago.

'The thing is Michael that Isolde has asked to come to the monastery here to learn to read and write.'

The priest shook his head vehemently; he wasn't going to give his daughter up to the monastery, having her live away from him.

'No, Prior, I don't want that, I don't want her away from me, I nearly lost her once.'

And then thinking about it, 'And she's a girl, it wouldn't be possible for a girl to live here at the monastery, wouldn't be right.'

Gilbert adjusted his position, or perhaps defined more clearly the possibilities as this opposition was expressed.

'I don't think she needs to live here, just come here some days to learn to read and write. This is what she said she wanted to do.'

'Write, Prior, what would Isolde do with writing?'

Prior Gilbert got up and walked across to the window and looked out onto the place where vegetables were grown and were two of the younger members of the monastery were supposed to be working but were actually fooling about. He knocked on the window, and they looked up at him and waved. Not the respect, the response required of a prior. He sighed; here was another problem that refused to go away.

He turned back to the priest hunched on the stool.

'The point is although we can't prove a miracle, Isolde has been saved, God has chosen to protect her, there is likely a particular task he will want her to do.'

'But she's only five, too small for tasks!'

This interjection was ignored.

'We need to make sure she is ready, is educated to enable her to do whatever it is that God wishes her to do. She doesn't need to be here all the time, just come down to the monastery when the tide is right, perhaps twice a week for her lessons.'

'But Prior Gilbert, how could she manage the journey?'

'Well, she has that big dog to protect her and perhaps she comes with Marjorie – I hear Marjorie is a very good cook, she could help out in the kitchen. And' – the prior was warming to the idea – 'perhaps there might be a donkey we could give her so she could ride down to Holy Island.'

Reflecting later on the situation, Gilbert realised the donkey had probably been the element that had secured the deal. A donkey was a valuable animal, the priest would realise that when not used to transport Isolde to Holy Island, the donkey would be available for community use.

Chapter Five

Prior Gilbert and Brother Gregory were holding their weekly Friday meeting after matins which reviewed monastery matters from the previous week and those that would need to be tackled over the next.

They had touched briefly on tithe payments without coming to any valid conclusion on how to deal with Sir Alan de Hetton's failure to pay his corn tithes and the situation in Lowick, the one chapel which constantly failed to produce the tithe payment due in October; it was now November. Gilbert mentioned his conversation with the Lowick Priest Michael, an example he said, of the problem for the church representative, a man of the church but living as part of the community. Spoke up for the difficult situation in which the priests found themselves, always Gilbert thought supporting those in difficulty, sometimes feeling he understood too well the suffering taking place, wishing he could be less involved, able as the other monks appeared to be, to treat the suffering of others as something inevitable, didn't Jesus say the poor are always with you.

They ended the session as always with a prayer and Brother Gregory then, left to go about his daily duties. However, just as Gilbert was wondering with which of the many tasks he should now engage, Brother Gregory had returned.

'Prior Gilbert, I think you should come and see.' He led him to where a window in the corridor looked out onto the courtyard. There was a man there having just dismounted from his horse, standing looking at the monastery building with the air of someone who hadn't been there for some time. Standing beside the man and horse was a small boy.

Gilbert recognised him immediately, turned to Brother Gregory for confirmation, Gregory nodded.

'Sir Alan de Hetton.'

And Gilbert said, 'I thought I would never see him here again, hoped through the mercy of our Lord Jesus that this would never happen. That he should dare after what he did, show his face here.'

'Not I think come to pay his tithes for this year.'

Gregory left him alone, turning down the corridor which led away from the monastery entrance to avoid an encounter.

How many years ago, 10, 12 there had been the incident on one of those occasions when the prior came up from Holy Island to take Eucharist in the chapel of Lowick. A terrible occasion he remembered vividly, probably the very worst thing that had ever happened to him.

In the middle of the Eucharist service just before the distribution of the host, the bread for communion, Gilbert began to hear noises coming from outside the chapel. The noises grew louder; there was now shouting and the sounds of conflict, something very unusual and troubling taking place outside in the churchyard. However much he tried to ignore what was happening outside, he was unable to do so as the sounds became louder and there was growing restlessness

40

among the congregation in the chapel. They were distracted, failing to follow his words, beginning to look back down the aisle to the door of the chapel as though at any moment the disturbance might spill out into the nave of the church. Some even began to leave to see what was going on outside, returning to tell others in excited whispers, the news spreading through the chapel like the tide racing in over the sands.

The service finally over, Prior Gilbert in full robes processed slowly down the aisle of the chapel followed by his cross bearer and two of his monks, trying hard to maintain the stately pace expected of a prior conducting his role as a spiritual leader of the church and community but aware of the congregation almost pushing behind him in their eagerness to see for themselves what was taking place outside.

The scene he discovered still gave him nightmares.

Sir Alan de Hetton mounted on his horse was facing the door of the chapel, surrounded by a group of his followers armed with clubs and cudgels. A number of injured persons: the prior's servants, his own followers, lying on the ground clutching injured head or arms.

There was total silence as the congregation observed the scene around them, and then they turned as one to look up at Sir Alan on his horse, waiting expectantly for the pronunciation that must follow.

On a quiet command from the knight, the horse advanced a few stately paces to bring Sir Alan immediately in front of the prior. The crowd of the congregation standing around him, observing the scene, were transfixed by these unusual circumstances, waiting to see what was going to happen.

'Prior Gilbert, you will see' – and here he gestured with a gauntleted hand at the scene around them – 'I have taken control of the churchyard. Some of my followers are at this moment chasing back your treasurer to where he belongs, at the monastery. And your horse, the fine palfrey you rode to come here has, I'm afraid disappeared, I fear you may have to walk back over the sands to your abbey.'

There was suppressed laughter.

He addressed now the members of the congregation:

'I have come here today people of Lowyk because I refuse to pay the corn tithes, this man' – pointing at Gilbert – 'and his monastery will have us pay, I cannot and will not pay them.'

There was murmured agreement from the assembled villagers.

'And now that I have made my position clear, I must leave.' And he turned his horse and trotted back towards the gate of the churchyard, his followers running behind him.

Nobody moved, watching the departing Sir Alan and his followers until they had disappeared out of sight. Then there was the noise of earnest discussion as the men gathered in groups to talk about what had happened, what they had seen and heard.

Prior Gilbert was ignored standing in his robes in front of the door to the chapel with his faithful cross bearer behind him. There was no sign of the two young monks who must have decided to use the confusion of the occasion to disappear from the scene.

Help was given to the injured servants and a horse and cart found to take them and the prior and cross bearer back to the monastery but this took time and lengthy negotiations were needed. Some, only a few, thought Gilbert as he sat beside the driver of the cart as they headed down the hill towards Holy Island, had stayed loyal to the church, showed they were shocked and unhappy at the action that had been taken.

Why however, hadn't he answered Sir Alan, how was it possible that he didn't use the occasion to berate the knight for the sacrilege of riding into the churchyard – was it in fact sacrilege? And injuring his servants all these were the most serious kinds of misdemeanours which in certain circumstances, considering also the public refusal to pay the corn tithes due towards the upkeep of the monastery could certainly lead to excommunication, the casting out of a person from the protection of the church and with it the terrible consequences of being excluded from the comfort and blessing of paradise, the promise of Jesus to his faithful of eternal life.

And as the carthorse slowly plodded its way across the sands back to the island, Gilbert thought how much the incident had been a challenge to his authority, to his position, his personal position as Prior appointed by the Bishop and abbey at Durham, the authority of the monastery and church of which he was the proud representative in this wild and lawless part of North Northumberland, subject to all the problems and difficulties of being a frontier area at a time of constant raids and warfare. How this incident had seriously and perhaps irrevocably damaged his position and his authority, his ability to deliver the word of Jesus to the poor people who found themselves caught up in such terrible times, living awful lives compounded by poverty and disease.

He had turned to speak to his cross-bearer seated behind him, to question him on the incident, how he viewed what had happened and what it might mean for the monastery but the man had fallen asleep, the cross laid down on the floor of the cart where his injured servants were lying, still from time to time groaning from their injuries.

These most vivid memories of certainly the worst day of his life as Prior were interrupted by the arrival of the person who had caused the distress. The door opened revealing Sir Alan de Heton, a slightly older form certainly with some grey hair but the same person none the less.

The knight pulled shut the door behind him and advanced towards the Prior seated at his desk, with a hand outstretched in greeting and bearing the smile of someone renewing a friendship after the intervention of a long passage of time. Prior Gilbert paused a moment before accepting the handshake.

'Prior Gilbert, I don't believe I need to introduce myself. You will, I'm sure, remember the incident in which we were involved many years ago and for which...' Here he sat himself down in front of the Prior's desk.

'I would like to apologise, sincerely apologise for my behaviour all those distant years ago. Difficult times, very difficult times for me and I had then the belief that immediate action was needed to rectify any given situation. And this matter of the payment of tithes, together with my terrible temper – which you will be pleased to hear has become much improved – drove me to react in a manner which I now accept was unacceptable from a knight and Christian. Behaviour towards an officer of the church, the prior of our venerable monastery here on Holy Island.'

'And the point is' – and here he looked directly at Prior Gilbert – 'You did not severely punish me for my behaviour, understood that then as now there were situations here in this unhappy border country which make all the ordinary conditions and ways of life far more complicated.'

Prior Gilbert was watching the man carefully, thinking how there should have been more serious punishment given the nature of the crimes committed, one of his servants had been permanently injured but mostly wondering just what had led Sir Alan to come to the monastery this morning, unlikely that this was about paying the corn tithes (that still remained unpaid) and wondering how long it would take for this preamble to be completed and the real purpose of the visit to be revealed.

'And so, Prior Gilbert, I have come to you this morning with a particular request. I have brought with me my son Alan de Hetton and would like you to take him into your monastery here that he might learn to behave like a Christian – he is a fearfully disobedient child, with a temper perhaps matching his father's previous disposition but nevertheless a good boy of whom I am...' – there was a pause – '...very fond and expect great things, and also, that he might learn to read and write.'

There it was now, placed out in the open for all to hear, his son to be put in the monastery, instructed by the monks in order to become able to read and write and behave like a Christian!

Prior Gilbert remained silent a moment considering the request, the impact the young, possibly difficult boy, might have on the life of the small monastery under his nominal control. There was of course the question of Isolde who would also be instructed at the monastery but not until after Michaelmas and she would not be living in the monastery. Also, there was the question of payment.

Before any concerns or conditions could be expressed, Sir Alan produced from his belt a leather pouch which he laid on the prior's desk without saying anything but the draw strings were untied and three gold coins fell on the desk.

'I would like him to start immediately.'

'And his name?'

'He is called: Alan, Michael, Tristan de Hetton.'

The prior had picked up a pen and was in the process of writing down the name but now paused.

'Tristan de Hetton?'

'Yes, Prior, named after an uncle of mine.'

'And where is your son, this Alan, Michael, Tristan de Hetton?'

'Waiting outside the door here as instructed.'

Sir Alan abruptly stood up and walked to the door which he opened revealing a small boy standing there, a look of bewilderment on his face as though unsure exactly of what was going to take place.

Sir Alan led the boy forward until he was standing directly in front of Prior Gilbert's desk.

'This Alan is Prior Gregory, the abbot of this monastery and a good man; you will do as he says.'

The boy looked from his father to the prior without saying anything, a look of anguish on his face.

'I am leaving you here in Prior Gregory's care. You will learn to be a good Christian here, to obey your instructions; to learn to read and write. And then after four years you will leave here to go to be a page, working with a knight at Norham

Castle, learning the military skills you will need as a knight, which I believe you wish to become.' Here he looked down at the boy a moment without receiving any response from him, for the boy was now staring straight ahead.

And then in a more conciliatory tone bending down towards the small figure of his son, he continued.

'You see to become a knight you have to have been a page Alan, and to be a page you have to read and write.'

'And to have Christian values.' This was Prior Gilbert.

Then whether because he had pressing business elsewhere or perhaps wanted to avoid a difficult departure, Sir Alan put a hand briefly on his son's shoulder before walking to the door which he opened, closing the door behind him as he went out into the corridor.

The young Alan had not moved since coming into the room, standing completely still, frozen into his position before the prior's desk staring straight ahead, his eyes fixed on the cross on the wall in front of him. Now at the sound of his father leaving, he suddenly turned his head, too late to see his father but in time to see the door shutting, closing from him everything familiar from a previous life now snatched from him, disappearing for ever. He looked a moment longer at the door, willing some sudden change, before turning back to stare at the wall, his apparent lack of emotion betrayed by the single tear falling down his cheek.

Prior Gilbert remembered his own experience of being left at the monastery at Durham aged just six, saying goodbye to his father outside the cathedral door with its frightening knocker. A memory and image that had stayed with him, his father trying to hide his emotion, the vast cathedral rising up beside them, handing across the small bag of belongings

Gilbert would take with him into this new life and then watching as his father after a quick embrace, hurried down the path away from him as the autumn leaves fell from the trees around them.

He turned to the boy.

'I want you to know, Alan, if you feel at any time frightened, lonely, you should come to find me. If in the middle of the night you awake and feel distressed, you should come to find me here in my office. I like to work through the night and will always be here if you need me. Do you understand?'

There was no response from the boy and Gilbert knew it was time to move things on and he collected Alan and brought him with him out into the corridor explaining they would need to go together to find Brother Gregory and a room for Alan to sleep in.

Chapter Six

Alan de Hetton, lay in his cot in the tiny room they had given him at the monastery, he was on his own, felt lonely and isolated, couldn't sleep. Around him in the dark was an unknown world, with smells and sounds different to anything he was used to. He thought about his home, his father, the servants he had known all his life; his animals, the dog Badger that slept at the end of his bed and followed him around everywhere. And thinking about Badger made him cry, how the poor animal would be missing him, could see the dog wandering around the house trying to find his master and then, sleeping on his own, beside the empty bed. He started to cry and couldn't stop himself, wailing for the poor animal and all the familiar things that had vanished from his life.

Alan with great effort forced himself to think of other things, told himself that this was not the behaviour of someone who would one day become a knight: Sir Alan, Michael, Tristan de Hetton. He lay there without moving, trying to feel braver, waiting to fall asleep, banishing from his mind any thoughts of home. But he couldn't sleep and so he made the mistake of getting out of bed and opening the wooden shutters on the single small window in his room to look outside.

It was dark outside, a view of a corner of the monastery wall with some large shrubs. He heard the sound of what he knew must be the sea making him realise he was unable now to cross back and go home, he was trapped here, on the island. Riding across the sands that morning with his father, he noticed the wet sand, the pools of water, showing where the sea had been, before withdrawing to somewhere unknown, where surely there must be terrible creatures, and knowing the sea must come back, as it had now. He shivered not from the cold, he told himself but from these thoughts that came to him out from the surrounding darkness.

He stopped suddenly, listening, straining to hear, there was a new sound, a strange and terrible wailing that seemed to be coming closer with the incoming sea. He looked out into the darkness and was shocked to see the bushes beside the monastery wall bend forward suddenly as though something was coming out from there to get him, Devils come to seek out unbelievers, coming to get him Alan de Hetton for being here at this monastery where he didn't belong. Fear took hold of him enveloping him, wrapping itself around him, so he froze petrified, unable to move. Only a sense of preservation made him give out a long, agonised scream as he turned, racing out of the room and away down the corridor, looking behind him as he ran, expecting to see the devils coming closer, gathering to smother him.

Alan didn't know where he was going only that he had to get away, escape. And then running down a long corridor, he noticed a light at the far end, coming from under a closed door. Reaching the light, he threw open the door and ran in, coming to an abrupt halt as he saw Prior Gilbert standing there looking surprised.

'Coming to get me, terrible bad things, devils, Prior,' he blurted out the message and pointed behind him the way he had just come. Then stood there gasping for breath, a look of terror on his face.

'Well, we had better close the door to keep them out Alan, Michael, Tristan de Hetton.' And Prior Gilbert put a reassuring hand on his shoulder as he went to shut the door, then brought the boy to the chair in front of the fire.

'I was just having my refreshments which help me to work through the nights. We have some milk and bread and honey. Would you like some Alan?'

The boy nodded and let out a sudden sob, before settling down to drink the milk from a flagon and eat the bread and honey, licking his fingers as the honey ran down them. Then looking up at the prior and saying.

'I heard this noise coming from the dark night, coming from the sea.'

'What kind of noise, Alan?'

'A wailing noise, Prior.' And here the boy shook his head as though trying to drive out the sounds from his ears and his mind.

Prior Gilbert lent back in his chair.

'Not devils, Alan, but seals, they sit out on the sandbanks and it's like singing, praising the Good Lord for their lives in a sea full of fishes.'

Alan looked unconvinced, eying the prior uncertainly before taking another long drink of the milk, beginning to feel warmer and calmer. Perhaps they weren't devils, just seals, and he tried to remember if he knew what a seal looked like.

'Now what are we going to do with you, Alan, I don't think you are ready to return to your room, so I think we should find you a story something from the Bible which will drive away bad thoughts, bringing you to the comforting narratives of those who have gone before worshipping and praising the good Lord Almighty.'

And he chooses Noah and the great flood as a suitable tale, able to engage a frightened small boy with its story of the arc and the animals and its lesson of salvation from an evil and sinful world.

He later took Alan back to his room and then, returned to his desk going back to what he had been doing prior to Arthur's entry: a study of the Book of Job, the relationship between God and those he forced to suffer, a suitable lecture for the current time of trouble they were all suffering.

It came to him to wonder how Alan would take to having another scholar working with him in the scriptorium, a younger girl Isolde.

Chapter Seven

You hear them before you see them. There is the sound of intermittent singing, someone laughing, the murmur of conversation drifting up on the light wind this clear spring morning. Then, they come into view heading down the track leading from Lowyk towards Holy Island a group of perhaps fifteen pilgrims, making their way slowly and painfully, like a band of soldiers returning from battle, ragged, many unwell having to stop every so often to lean on a staff to catch their breath, before limping on; some are barefoot to give more credence to their penance, more force to their humility. Young and old, the elder members of the group needing support as they follow this final day of a pilgrimage that has brought them from the north and west, highland places in the distant depths of Scotland and south down the Devil's Causeway; all coming to seek help and guidance, a cure for their ailments or distress, forgiveness for their sins through this act of pilgrimage to the island of the blessed Saint Cuthbert.

Those from north of the border are wary as they walk through this border area which has suffered raids and destruction from their countrymen. Although pilgrims are protected, it doesn't mean they will be well treated by those who have felt the full impact of the long conflict, death and maiming, the torching of homes and stealing of cattle.

As they come closer, you can make out the individuals see the fatigue etched on faces from a long, difficult journey through uncertain weather but there is also in their eyes, a sense of purpose, an anticipation of resolution, the hope their prayers will be answered.

A young girl with a baby is riding amongst them and beside her, the small figure of Isolde who has offered the girl a ride on the donkey intended for her journey to lessons at the monastery. Marjorie Grubbe and Fortune, walk behind the donkey, the pilgrims keeping a respectful distance from the large dog. Marjorie, famous for her soup, is employed on these twice weekly sessions to prepare lunch for the Prior and monks.

Isolde is known to the pilgrims, pointed out as someone special for her story has been told to explain a child's presence here among them, how she is somehow blessed, someone chosen for a particular task since her miraculous saving from the rising tide on this same causeway they are about to cross, the most difficult and dangerous part of the whole journey. It feels comforting to have her with them.

The pilgrims have left Lowyk early that morning, told there is only a three and a half hour journey to the island. They have chosen a guide in the village to take them because only a guide will be able to show them which track to safely take across the sands and the correct time to travel. A price has been negotiated with the guide, a surly man name Wilfred who is walking ahead of them, constantly urging them to keep up.

There is a hill to climb and the pilgrims burst into song again, competing with the larks, tiny specks hovering high above them. Wilfred waits impatiently for the group to come together, then leading them off the track and along a worn path, as the ground rises up before them. A younger pilgrim realising what this must mean, runs up the path before shouting out in excitement, as others follow more slowly to where the view opens up in front of them.

Everything is sea and sky with the long, low shape of the island, Holy Island, there is smoke drifting up from the small cluster of houses that make up the village and beyond the monastery buildings with the magnificent priory church they have journeyed towards for the past weeks, a place many were afraid they would never see.

Some of the pilgrims are crying, many fall to their knees.

A tall man takes control.

'We must give our thanks to the Almighty for bringing us safely here to Mount Joy and our first view of Holy Island.'

Then in a strong Scot's voice as the pilgrims kneel, he forms the words of prayer, weighting carefully each word spoken slowly, as though giving time for each phrase to be offered up to the sea and island and the heavens above them.

'Blessed Cuthbert,

Thank you for bringing us here

Safely to view the place of your ministry,

Where so many miracles have been created in your name.

Help us as we end this long pilgrimage

To attain salvation

The salvation we are desperately seeking.'

'Amen.'

They then relax, sitting down to take in the view, pointing out to each other, the causeway they will soon be crossing and the long track between the marsh and sand-dunes they will have to take before coming to the village and then the monastery beyond. There is still a good way to go.

Wilfred chooses this moment to stand in front of them partially blocking out the view.

'To make the crossing, you have more to pay.'

There is an angry murmur from the pilgrims.

A number of voices speak out in protest, saying how this had already been decided that no further payment was expected.

'We've already paid; paid you to take us to Holy Island, crossing the sands was part of this.' This is the leader who has stepped forward to talk to him, his face red with anger.

'Well, this is how it is; you want to move from here down this hill and across the dangerous sands to the monastery.' He turns and points out each part of the journey on the landscape in front of them.

Then, turns back to confront them with his repeated demand.

'You're going to have to pay more or I shall leave you here.'

And he turns away, taking bread from his bag which he begins to chew. This argument is familiar to him, this moment pilgrims realise they have been cheated but know there is little they can do about it. They need a guide, can't safely cross the causeway without one, it's too dangerous. It is for him a moment of satisfaction, enabling him to show who is in control.

The pilgrims look at one another, they want to cross over the sands now, don't want to wait any longer, don't want to wait another day for the tide to be right. Some begin to sort out coins to pay him, others stand there defiant but there is a distraction.

They become aware of Isolde walking back up from the edge of the field where the donkey has been grazing. She has a bunch of primroses in her hand which she has just picked, perhaps to give to the prior and she walks towards Wilfred, people make way for her until she is in front of the guide.

It is not clear what will happen next. It seems that Isolde is also unsure what to do; she keeps looking down from the flowers to the guide standing with his back to her, the pilgrims grouped around them.

Wilfred realises something is happening, can sense in the silence everyone is waiting for something. He doesn't want to, but finds himself turning to see what is happening, what has led to this sudden change.

The small child is standing there holding the flowers, watching him.

The guide gazes at her, then narrows his eyes to observe the pilgrims watching him, realising this small child is challenging his authority, that there is a danger he will lose control that the money he makes from acting as a guide is being compromised. He should ignore her, carry on as though she isn't standing there, pretending he believes the flowers are not for him and makes to move away.

But the girl is persistent walking closer, making it clear she wants to give the flowers to him. Some would later claim that she said something, others that she had shaken her head but for most nothing was spoken.

For a long time nothing happens. There is something important about this moment standing on Mount Joy, with Holy Island, the place they had travelled so far to come to, in front of them. It would be difficult to refuse the flowers or later throw them away once they had been accepted. In some way, it seemed that it would not be easy to continue to demand more payment once the flowers had been taken from the girl, had been accepted. As though by accepting the flowers, the guide would have become a person showing greater understanding, sympathy for the plight of the pilgrims he was escorting.

The girl comes closer pushing the flowers towards him, urging him to take them, there is no expression on her face. Someone said later that it was as though she was forcing him to take them that there was somehow an obligation to accept them.

The guide muttered something, wiped his hands on his smock before taking the flowers from the small hand. The flowers are crumpled from being clutched tightly in the small fist some of the pale-yellow primroses and crinkly green leaves, fell as she handed them to him and she stoops to pick them up to add to the bunch he was already holding.

The man said nothing, looked down at the primroses in his hand, then slowly moved back down the path clutching the bunch of flowers back down the path to the track as it headed down towards the island. Then, he turned and moved away from them, there is still the causeway and the length of the sacred island of Lindisfarne to cover before the group reach the monastery, their destination. The pilgrims following on behind him, thinking about what they had just seen, the sea charged land they had to cross and the monastery they would soon be approaching.

Chapter Eight

Isolde dipped the quill pen into the ink, taking great care not to spill the liquid and formed the capital "S", enjoying the movement made to shape the letter, the curving form it made as it joined the line of "s" on the small piece of parchment she had been allowed, as a great privilege, to use. She put her pen down on the desk and admired her work, the form of the letter reminding her of the snake she had seen, one sunny evening as the leaves were turning, how it had lain there on the warm rock, watching her, black skin, a male snake which people said was the most dangerous.

She hadn't been afraid, other children she knew would have cried out, run away or shouted for help, perhaps thrown rocks at this evil creature that could kill. The snake that had told Eve to eat the apple of good and evil which had cast her and Adam out of paradise, it was unlucky to see a snake, danger lurking in the grass ready to attack you, children from Lowyk had died from being bitten by snakes.

There was just this shared moment, the girl and the snake watching each other and waiting to see what would happen. Then after a long moment, the snake had slithered away, she watched it disappear into the bracken.

When she told others what had happened, they said she hadn't been attacked because she was a special person, chosen by Saint Cuthbert and that it was Blessed Saint Cuthbert who had protected her as he had saved her before from drowning as the tide came rushing in.

She picked up the pen again and began to write underneath more letters; only this time there was a word, the "S" heading the word "Sanctus". Isolde didn't like being special, she wanted to be like everyone else, people, old people would come to ask her advice and children no longer played with her because she was different. She had no friends.

Brother Gregory came in and came over to her, looking over her shoulder, smiling and nodding when he saw how well she was doing. She liked Brother Gregory, he didn't talk much but he was kind and helped her, showed her how to form the letters.

'And your friend Alan de Hetton, he is not here this morning?'

'No, Brother Gregory, I haven't seen him. He doesn't like to be here in the scriptorium, wants to be outside. He isn't my friend!'

Alan de Hetton was eight, three years older than Isolde and wasn't her friend. The two of them shared lessons in the scriptorium but he didn't like her. He would kick and punch her when the monks weren't looking, try to spoil her work and play tricks on her, hiding her pen.

Once with great daring Isolde had come up to him at the end of the lesson to ask:

'Why don't you like me, Alan?'

He hadn't even looked at her, when he didn't hurt her it was as though she didn't exist, he would look straight past her as though she wasn't present in the classroom. Isolde thought he was going to pretend she hadn't spoken that usually happened, when she said anything to him.

He had looked up from the scribbles he had made and seemed to think carefully about an answer, then turning to her, pointed aggressively and shouted:

'You're a girl!'

Smiling, pleased with his answer, Alan went back to what he was doing as Isolde made her way slowly back to her desk wishing she had never asked the question.

'How is Alan getting on with his writing?'

Brother Gregory shook his head in despair.

There was silence as they both considered the problem of Alan.

'He is of course his father's son.'

And they both remembered Sir Alan de Hetton's taking over of the Lowick church yard.

'Living with his father, no mother, the boy spending all his time with him, riding, hunting, a male household. Wenches.'

'Prior Gilbert, did you say wenches?'

'Did I speak that…I hadn't meant to, I must apologise at the use of such a "gros mot", I was thinking of the young females Sir Alan is known to bring back to Hetton Hall.' And the two old monks looked at one another laughing at this unexpected word from the mouth of a senior prelate.

Prior Gilbert thought it useful to change the subject at this point.

'I hear he is useful helping out with the animals, good with horses.'

Brother Gregory nodded.

'And then there is the problem of how he treats Isolde, Marjorie came to see me, complained about the bruises where Alan had punched and kicked her. We have to find a way to improve the situation with Alan and Isolde.'

'Prior Gilbert, you have soon to go to Durham for the meeting with the Bishop?'

Gilbert nodded.

'You will need someone to go with you, why don't you take Alan; you need someone to look after the horses.'

Gilbert considered this a moment. 'He is very young. Perhaps giving him responsibility would help, something he would respond to, enjoy.'

Their conversation was interrupted by the arrival of one of the younger monks.

'Prior Gilbert, Isolde has gone missing and we think she has been locked in the scriptorium cupboard.' He bowed briefly having delivered this news and then disappeared.

Brother Andrew, Gilbert thought, watching him retire, one of the better young monks. He turned to Gregory to ask him to address the situation but Gregory was already making his way towards the scriptorium his face set.

She must have fallen asleep, woke now in the dark of the big wooden cupboard, remembering how Alan had said Brother Gregory wanted her to fetch more parchment from the cupboard and handed her the key. Then as she was looking in the cupboard for the parchment, had felt herself being pushed inside and heard the key being turned to lock her in. She had cried out and banged on the door but there was no response and she knew Brother Gregory had said he had to go to his meeting with Prior Gilbert, how if they needed anything, they should go and find Brother Andrew.

Isolde wasn't frightened, knew someone would come to find her. The cupboard was large enough for a small person to lie down and so she had made herself comfortable lying on a pile of old vestments. She fell asleep again wondering how Alan would be punished.

She was woken by the sound of voices, Brother Gregory's deep voice and the distinctive sound of a smack with a yelp from Alan.

'Key, fetch the key boy, go!' And the sound of Alan running off and a long pause; waiting for him to return. Perhaps, Isolde thought, he has thrown the key away.

Isolde wondered how much longer she would be in the cupboard and what they would do if the key couldn't be found, then, everything happened quickly. Alan returned, the key was turned in the lock, the door to the cupboard swung open as Isolde immerged blinking from the sudden brightness.

She sat on the floor watching as Brother Gregory caught hold of Alan as he stepped back from the cupboard, hoisting him off the ground and holding him at arm's length with one hand to avoid Alan's kicking legs as he struggled to free himself making Isolde smile, he looked silly.

Brother Gregory looked down at her to see if she was all right and Isolde nodded. He let go of Alan who fell on the floor in front of her, his face blank. Slowly rising to his feet trying to avoid a further possible blow from Brother Gregory who shouted at him:

'Go tell Prior Gilbert what you have done!'

Isolde watched as Alan hurried out of the room to find Prior Gilbert, wondering what the punishment would be and whether this would help her.

Alan came to the Prior's door, remembering the many times he had arrived here in the middle of the night, frightened by the terrors of the dark of the bible stories that had comforted him, all of which seemed a very long time ago.

What he wondered would Prior Gilbert do, how would he punish him? Probably beat him and then send him home to his father which looking at the old wooden door in front of him seemed a good thing to happen, leave this awful place with lessons and learning and Brother Gregory and the monks and the girl. Then he thought how his father would react. Alan decided it would be better not to leave the monastery.

He knocked and because no one answered slowly opened the door. Prior Gilbert was standing looking out of the window; he didn't turn or acknowledge Alan's presence.

Alan waited a moment before deciding to speak.

'Prior Gilbert, I have to tell you something...something bad.'

There was no response, so after a further pause Alan continued.

'You see, I locked the girl in the cupboard.'

'Which girl?'

'The girl' – he shook his head not knowing what she was called and continued with his confession – 'locked her in the cupboard in the scriptorium' – and feeling the need to provide further information now he had admitted his crime – 'and left her there all alone in the dark,' to show he appreciated the full horror of his beastly behaviour.

The Prior remained looking out of the window, there was no response.

'Prior Gilbert, you should beat me.'

This made Gilbert conceal a smile, he turned to look at the small boy in front of him.

'Alan, Michael, Triston de Hetton, I am not going to beat you. I'm going to give you a task.'

Alan wasn't very sure what a task represented, wouldn't a beating be better, he had had plenty of beatings. He was watching Prior Gilbert carefully, waiting to hear what it was he had to do, what a task would mean.

'You have kicked and punched and found all kinds of ways to upset Isolde.'

'And locked the girl in a cupboard,' Alan reminded him.

Now and for the only time since Alan had come to the monastery, Prior Gilbert raised his voice in anger, shouting at him.

'And you don't even know her name! It's Isolde, Alan the daughter of the priest of Lowyk, the girl is called Isolde!'

Alan hung his head at this unexpected and uncharacteristic anger from the Prior.

Prior Gilbert sighed; perhaps this task would be impossible, so he sat down at his desk. He had been pleased to have children at the monastery, it made a difference but it wasn't working and if Isolde remained unhappy, he could see her leaving. Marjorie had told him this.

'What I want you to do, Alan, is become friends with Isolde.' And as he said this, it sounded a hopeless task, one that could never happen.

There was a long pause as Alan thought about this, before asking: 'Is this the task, Prior Gilbert?'

Gilbert nodded and for a moment he thought Alan was going to refuse, ask to be beaten instead. There was about the boy though something earnest, a wish to please and from those middle of the night sessions when he had read of Noah and the battles of the Israelites, Bible readings to comfort someone missing his home and terrified of the new place he had come to, Gilbert had become fond of the boy, maybe, just maybe this could work.

The boy spoke: 'What would I have to do to become her friend?'

'It's not going to be easy, as she's frightened of you of what you might do to her. It's going to take time for her to realise she can trust you. Watch her, see what she likes, how she behaves, help her, slowly try to become friends.'

There was another pause as Alan visibly thought through this, before he looked up at the Prior.

'Yes, I will do this, become the girl's friend' – and quickly to avoid the Prior Gilbert's anger, corrected himself – 'Isolde's friend.' And he nodded, smiling as he turned away to walk from Prior's room to begin the task.

Gilbert watched him leave, realising that Alan was not someone who could ever wait but needed everything to happen straight away.

Isolde watched as Alan returned to the scriptorium, she noticed he wasn't crying, was looking at her as he came towards her. This was not something that had happened before, he had ignored her. He went back to his desk behind her from where he had thrown things when Brother Gregory wasn't watching. Was he smiling?

Brother Gregory was also watching Alan's return and now got up and left the room, perhaps going to see the prior to find out what had happened.

'Girl!'

Isolde ignored his calling her.

He repeated the word: 'Girl!'

'My name is Isolde,' said without turning.

'Yes, I know, Isolde,' he said the word carefully, as though trying it out for the first time as he spoke to her.

'Isolde, Prior Gilbert wants me be to be friends with you.'

At the end of the morning's lessons, Alan usually left in a hurry to go to the horses but this morning he followed her into the refectory, watching her collect her apple, the lump of bread and cheese, taking the same.

They walked out together and sat down outside on the grass where there was a view of the blue sea. They ate in silence, Isolde wondering what was going to happen, not happy with this new Alan, waiting for the old Alan to surface again with some kind of trick or sudden reaction to her. After a while he said, 'I don't know what it means to be a friend?'

She looked at him thinking this was a way to get her to say something, so he could make fun of her, shout at her. How did anyone not know what being a friend was like? He looked serious, was watching her, waiting for a response which made her nervous.

'What does a friend have to do?'

She got up to walk away, to avoid what she was sure was coming next.

'Please, Isolde, you see I don't know, don't know about friends.'

So, she didn't walk away but stood there a moment before answering, speaking without looking at him to avoid what she was sure would be his smirking face.

'I think a friend helps you, looks after you, is with you when you are sad, I don't have any friends.'

Then, she walked quickly away back inside the monastery to practice her writing. He hadn't followed her and she paused at the big wooden door to look back, Alan hadn't moved, was still sitting there the uneaten apple in his hand looking out to sea.

Chapter Nine

Prior Gilbert and Alan rode side by side along the Devil's Causeway, the sound of their horses' hooves beating out a pleasant rhythm on the paved road as they headed south towards Durham.

The empty Roman road stretched out before them like an unfolding narrative, inviting this movement forward away from daily routines, the pressing issues of the everyday. It was a bright autumn morning, the trees beside the road just turning to the seasonal reds and golds; it was good Gilbert thought, to be here, now at this moment.

He turned to his young companion to see whether Alan shared the pleasure of this journey away from the monastery. There was a big smile and nod of the head, before the boy dug his spurs into his pony's flanks and galloped away up towards the brow of the hill, turning to survey the lie of the land there a moment, before riding back to his position beside Prior Gilbert. A process which punctuated their progress and that Gilbert was beginning to find tiresome, wondering whether he should dissuade him from this activity but not wanting to dampen his obvious enthusiasm.

'Bad place for robbers, Prior Gilbert, my father told me.' He waved his hand towards where woodland masked the road ahead. 'Ambush here you see, come out from the trees to rob you, take everything, even the horses.' And he looked down at his pony considering how they might deal with this.

Gilbert realised that Alan didn't see himself as just looking after the horses but also, as someone charged with protecting the Prior. Gilbert wasn't sure how the boy could possibly help, knowing it would be more a question of ensuring Alan didn't get himself in trouble and get hurt if anything did arise.

They had spent the previous night staying at Hetton Castle with Sir Alan de Hetton, Alan's father. The man was the perfect host, taking great care to look after the prior, providing his best food – venison and a good red wine.

Once the boy had retired to bed helped by one of the two beautiful ladies, described as distant cousins, who lived with Sir Alan, the two of them had attacked a further bottle of the claret, sitting beside the fire in the great chamber.

'Now, Prior, how is Alan getting on?'

Prior Gilbert accepted a refill before replying, sitting back comfortably in the armchair, thinking how he was treated here with more respect than at the monastery where, as prior, he deserved consideration that was not forthcoming. The man sitting in front of him who had given him more trouble in the past than anyone, was now treating him like someone of consequence and at the same time like an old friend because Gilbert supposed they had shared previous difficult situations and then, he was, charged with educating Sir Alan's son.

'Initially, I think Sir Alan he was a little unhappy. Didn't really want to be with us at the monastery on Holy Island, wasn't getting on very well with his lessons, wanted to be working with the animals.'

'But then that changed, a girl?'

Prior nodded, Sir Alan had, he realised been receiving brief, occasional letters from his son.

'Unusual situation, Sir Alan, we have a girl in the monastery, Isolde and she has been helping Alan, they have become good friends,' he congratulated himself on his part in the success of this matter but wondered how Sir Alan would see his son's friendship with a girl.

There was a pause as Sir Alan considered his response.

'Yes, I know about this, a good thing. There is nothing like the soft whispering presence of young ladies.' He helped himself to some more wine as he emphasised the point.

One of his "cousins" came to say at this point that his son was fast asleep, tossing her long hair back from her face as Sir Alan smiled at her. Gilbert found the word "wenches" came back to him from the conversation with Brother Gregory, making him smile again.

'You see, Prior, after my wife died, Alan's mother, and before my "cousins" came to stay, this was just a world of men and boys and dogs and horses, hunting and fighting' – looking up to explain this – 'whosoever needed fighting, strictly for defence you understand. No soft edges and I think for the boy this was a bad thing which is why I sent him to you, well of course also, the education.' A moment of silence followed as he considered the matter and "learning about the scriptures".

'He didn't know anything about girls had never come across any and so of course he had to learn how to treat them, wouldn't know you see; no experience.' Then, thoughtfully, 'I think you see we behave differently when women are around.'

A man appeared in the room, standing by the door without entering.

'Ah, the night watch, have to go to check we have no raiders about, that everything is as it should be, calm and peaceful. We live you know in terrible times.' He got up and put on his cloak, turning to Prior Gilbert as he did so.

'Do you want to join us? Just a question of going up onto the tower to watch, look over the surrounding area.'

Prior Gilbert followed them up a series of ladders, until a trap-door opened out onto the roof, wondering what they were actually going to see in the dark. A raised walkway around the edge of the tower meant it was possible to observe the countryside in every direction. He joined the other two as they stood in silence watching and listening.

It was a warm still night with just a slight breeze coming off the sea. There was the sound of an owl somewhere over by the wooded hills to the east which then went silent.

After a moment, Sir Alan turned to him.

'You see, Prior, it may be dark but you can sense from up here when anything seems wrong. There may be the sound of a horse – no one goes out at this time of night unless they have evil to do – or a moving light. You can tell too from the way birds or animals are disturbed when something is wrong.'

'What are you expecting?' Gilbert wasn't sure why he was whispering.

'Increasingly, there are Scot's raids – since Bannockburn – sometimes small parties of say 15 or 20 horse, on occasion much bigger groups, up to two hundred. Then of course you can hear them, see their lights. They take cattle, sometimes burn villages and take hostages demanding ransom.'

'So what action do you take?'

'Light the beacon, sound the alarm' – he pointed to the bell beside them – 'to warn the other villages and send out scouts to follow them. With the big groups, there is no way we can fight them, so we send for help from Norham.'

The man appeared beside them and pointed out into the dark. Gilbert could make nothing out but Sir Alan nodded.

'Poacher, out there by the wood, there was an owl calling, and now everything has gone silent, as though the animals are watching something.'

He nodded to the man, who disappeared quickly into the darkness.

'We know who it is; have had plenty of dealings with him. He has a large family to feed and goes out at night to find what he can I can't have my deer taken.'

Gilbert remembered that he hadn't wanted to ask what would happen to the poacher if he was caught. He was thinking about this conversation now, as they travelled down the Devil's Causeway towards Durham.

It was at this moment that he realised a man had stepped out from the side of the road just ahead, watching Alan, riding up away from them. Gilbert wasn't a man to overreact but was worried for Alan. His own horse moved forward, bringing him closer to the man.

He became aware at this point that someone had appeared from the other side of the road and was holding his bridle, bringing his horse to a halt.

Nobody said anything, their attention drawn to the piercing scream from Alan who realising there was a problem, was now galloping down the hill to Prior Gilbert's rescue, waving in the air what could only be a wooden sword. He directed his attention to the smaller of the two men standing in the road, presumably with the intention of knocking him over with the impact of the pony.

The man moved smartly to his left at the last moment to avoid the collision, at the same time as shooting out his staff to strike Alan in the chest, lifting the boy from his saddle and projecting him into the ditch.

They all watched as Alan picked himself up and without pausing, rushed at the man who had done this to him. Unable to take seriously the threat from this small boy, the man stood still with a smile on his face as Alan banged into him, knocking him off his feet then, suffering the indignity of being pummelled with a wooden sword.

There was a noise from the man holding the Prior's horse. Gilbert turned to look and was surprised to find he was roaring with laughter.

It took a moment for order to be restored as the first man brought Alan up to them, hands tied behind his back. He was shouting out a range of insults and warning the robbers of the consequences of their action and how his father Sir Alan de Hetton would wreak terrible vengeance on them.

The man holding the Prior's bridle stopped laughing.

'You are Sir Alan de Hetton's lad, boy?'

'Yes and he will not sleep until he has brought you and you' – with his hands tied, pointing his head at the two robbers – 'to a horrible punishment.'

The reaction to this was instant.

'Untie him, I know Sir Alan, I have battled Scots' raiders with him. He is a fearsome fighter, who all in this borderland knows and respects. We will let you both continue your journey without further trouble in honour of your father, boy.'

The first robber was sent to fetch Alan's pony and the boy helped to mount the animal, even his wooden sword returned to him.

They had only gone a yard or two when the leading robber called to them to stop. Prior Gilbert worrying there had been a change of plan.

'Sir, you are I believe a man of the church?'

'Yes, my name is Prior Gilbert from the monastery at Holy Island travelling on business to Durham.'

'Would you, Prior, do me a great favour, bless a poor man forced to commit robbery by the terrible circumstances in which he finds himself.'

'I don't think a pardon or forgiveness of sins is appropriate, given that you had the intention to rob and possibly harm us, I can however give you a simple blessing.' And here he signalled for the man to kneel.

'Almighty Father, look down on this poor man and despite his crimes and the misfortunes he has done to others, pity him for these offences and out of your great goodness help him to change his ways in order he lead in the future a better life. Amen.'

Prior Gilbert watched as the man rose to his feet, bowed his head in thanks, and then joined his fellow robber, disappearing back into the wood from whence they had come.

A story here, the Prior thought as they continued on their way south to Durham, a tale to tell to fellow monks on a winter's evening. He turned to check Alan was not damaged by this venture but the boy had already ridden off to search for further robbers, filled now with the confidence of his ability to protect the prior and proud of how the mere mention of his father's name had tamed the bad men.

It could all have been very different. The Prior Gilbert gave a prayer of thanks, it was difficult not to see the hand of God in their deliverance.

Chapter Ten

'You will all be aware of why I have brought you here for this convocation of priors from each of our beloved monasteries. As Lord Bishop of Durham, I have responsibility for you all and the blessed work you do in the name of our Holy Father the Lord Jesus Christ.

There are a number of matters to discuss with you during your short time here at Durham, such as the problems in the north of our diocese where continued conflict, unrest, deprivation and failing harvests have led to the non-payment of tithes.'

The great man paused here, looking directly at Prior Gilbert before continuing.

'Tithes which are essential, as you well know for the continued presence of our monasteries in these troubled areas.'

But here the Prince Bishop softened his approach nodding his great head and now smiling at Gilbert; they had known one another since both coming as boys to the monastery here at Durham so many years before. He raised his hand, causing the deep sapphire blue of his episcopal ring to flash in the sunlight, like a symbol of the man's authority and power to carry out God's work in this most northerly province of the most Holy Catholic Church in England.

'I realise Prior Gilbert how difficult these times are for you and understand with famine, there may be times when the tithes cannot be paid as has happened in recent years but we must maintain our monastery on Holy Island. Maintain this precious link with the Blessed Saint Cuthbert who led the conversion of pagans in the borders and whose body, following the terrible Viking raids, came, finally, after a long and dangerous journey to be buried here in our great cathedral.'

There was a murmur of agreement from the assembled priors.

'However, there is another and even more pressing need for me to speak to you this day and the reason for which we are gathered here this morning. You will all be aware of the terrible pestilence which is ravaging our country and even now comes ever nearer and is likely soon to fall amongst us here in the North with desperate consequences, bringing the death of the young and old, mothers and children, threatening the very fabric of our lives.'

There was silence here as Bishop Thomas looked down a moment, bringing his hands together in the position of prayer, allowing the true awfulness of the situation to infect them.

'Brother William will describe to you in a moment.' All turned to look at the tall ascetic looking man sitting on the right hand of the bishop as he was pointed out to them. 'The actions we will be taking to address this, the most serious crisis with which we or our fathers or our fathers' fathers have ever been challenged.'

Another pause to take a drink from the gold goblet on the table in front of him.

'Brother William has come to us from Lincoln, a man of great intellect and piety, a trained lawyer who has studied at Oxford and Bologna and whose ambition is to promote the work of the monasteries in our region. We are lucky to have him among us, particularly at the present difficult time.'

Brother William barely acknowledged this praise with only the slightest dip of his head, as he continued to look straight in front of him. Arrogance, thought Prior Gilbert, who took an instant dislike to him. In his experience, those ecclesiastical persons who combined intellect with piety and ambition often lacked a spiritual element, the ability to understand the problems of others.

'I want first to describe to you what this pestilence represents. You will want to ask yourselves and be able to respond to the frightened requests of those living within your jurisdiction.' And here he raised his voice.

'What have we done to deserve this affliction?'

The bishop looked down at the assembled priors, their anxious faces turned towards him, waiting for what he would say.

'My fellow monks, what we have done is nothing less than provoked the divine anger...by a just judgement to revenge.'

He let this settle before proceeding in a quieter voice.

'This is a just judgement because we deserve to be punished, punished for our beastly lives, our inability to follow the words of the scriptures, listen to the commandments of Moses and lead the just life of God fearing Christians. And so, we are going to be made to suffer – all of us, the rich and poor and even I fear members of the ecclesiastical body, who have failed in their duty as shepherds of their flocks.'

Bishop Thomas paused again to make sure the full horror of his words was being digested.

'The question is at this late hour, what can we do to respond to this coming agony?' The raising of the ecclesiastical voice now, turned to a roar of anger.

'Repent!'

He sat down to a shocked silence. Then, a murmur of concern flowed down the long, oak table, growing in volume as the Priors turned to their neighbours, reacting to these pronouncements.

It was a moment before they realised that Brother William was now on his feet ready to address them, waiting impatiently. He brought his fist down on the table and there was instant silence. Pausing a moment to ensure he had every one of them watching him, he spoke slowly giving each word authority.

'We will repent be very assured my Lord Bishop. From each of our monasteries in every one of our churches, we will organise Penitentia Processions, gatherings of all those living in every town and village within our area to humbly walk to an appointed place of worship: cathedral, monastery, parish church or chapel where we will most earnestly pray for forgiveness.'

'But' – he gave the word full force – 'understand that those who die from the pestilence will have the gates of paradise slammed shut before them, for they are being punished by God for their sins and will suffer horribly not just from the pains of pestilence but also, from the eternal suffering of the damnation of hell. There is in the pestilence a necessary cleansing, destroying all that is evil and unacceptable in the sight of God, so new beginnings can be made.'

'Possibly' – here a slight change in tone – 'just possibly, some of those gathered there who repent of their useless lives and heinous crimes will be spared the dreadful horrors of the pestilence and will be able to look forward to the indescribable pleasures of paradise, the garden from where Adam and Eve were banished for their sins.'

Prior Gilbert was sitting at table enjoying the candlelight supper prepared for the Priors which he was pleased to see had not been tainted with a concern to match the need for piety in this difficult time by reducing the food to lent proportions and content. It was good to meet up here with old friends, to talk of the past and discuss common problems they encountered as priors. There seemed an unwillingness to dwell on the words that had been spoken that morning, and to leave aside any talk of the coming pestilence that would be soon upon them.

A servant interrupted his account of Sir Alan de Hetton's misadventures and handed him a note which he found was written in French while Latin was known to all, French had become a more unusual form of address and one that protected any missive from the unwanted attention of others.

The note came from Bishop Thomas:

Mon Cher Ami,
Que les jours s'en vont!
La chance de vous rencontrer ce soir,

a huit heures dans mon parloir sera fort
utile et un grand plaisir.

Thomas

Prior Gilbert recognised the writing although, perhaps now slightly more assured to match his current position of authority.

It took Prior Gilbert a moment to find the Bishop's parlour wandering down a series of long, dark corridors until he finally came to a substantial door which he recognised from previous visits. A figure came out of the door, hurrying back down the corridor without acknowledging him. It was only after he had disappeared that Gilbert realised this had been Brother William.

Bishop Thomas greeted him and with a hand on his shoulder ushered him into the pleasant parlour, a room lit by a large candelabrum above a table covered in parchments of various sizes. Beyond the table a fire was burning. Gilbert noticed the dark oak panelling, a number of small tapestries with religious themes and a jewelled cross on the wall which he remembered from coming here as a young monk.

A steward arrived with a jug of wine from a door at the far end of the room, the bishop raised a hand.

'Peter, I think we need something rather better for the Prior of Holy Island, do we have any of the burgundy left?'

'Yes, my Lord.' And the man disappeared again.

'Now Gilbert, my friend, a pleasure to see you, it has been a long time. Make yourself comfortable here in front of the fire.'

'Brother William seemed to be in a hurry.'

'He didn't get what he wanted.'

Gilbert knew that it would not be politic to pursue this further. Bishop Thomas was known for his sudden outbursts of temper, whenever he felt his authority was challenged or when questioned about ecclesiastical business. It was unwise to forget, despite their long friendship, that this was the Prince Bishop, a man of considerable authority. The bishop, however, chose to clarify the situation.

'You see Prior Gilbert, although as Prince Bishop I appear to have every authority, should a person of importance in the kingdom decide they wanted to place someone here at the monastery of Durham, to be given a position of authority and a task to complete, it would be unwise for me to refuse, you will understand, patronage is of great importance.'

He considered a moment. 'Although if this person did something unwelcome, I would have no hesitation in sending him back from where he came.'

Here however, Bishop Thomas decided to move to other matters.

'Now, Prior Gilbert, distract me from Brother William and monastery business, the coming pestilence and Scotch matters. Recount again the tales of that wondrous summer in Normandy when two young monks were sent to Rouen to learn French.'

He looked at Gilbert.

'How many years ago now, 35?'

'Yes, my Lord Bishop.'

'I don't remember their names?'

'Geraldine and Sophie.'

'Blonde hair, large smiles.'

The steward, Peter, returned with a large jug of burgundy which he poured out for them into the goblets on the small tables beside each chair.

The steward left and they sat in silence a moment drinking the wine which Gilbert realised was probably the best he had ever tasted.

'I want you to tell me the story, Prior, how it was, you have a better memory than me.'

Prior Gilbert took a further drink of the wine, confirming its excellence.

Bishop Thomas was looking at him carefully.

'You can still remember all the details?'

Gilbert nodded smiling; this was why he was here this was his task. They would come to business matters later.

'I want to hear the story again, to imagine being a young monk of 17, I want you to take me from this Durham Cathedral to one hot, June morning in France.'

He closed his eyes and sat back in his armchair clutching the goblet of burgundy in both hands as though the red liquid it contained, helped confer the warmth of memories.

'Somehow, we managed to get a free morning and walked out of Rouen monastery into the town. It was a hot morning.'

The bishop nodded.

'Finding ourselves in the "place du Marché", we wanted to practice our French. There were the two young girls.'

'Geraldine and Sophie.'

'Yes, selling fruit from their Normandy farm, I remember cherries and apricots and peaches, we were joking with them, asking the prices and then you, Bishop Thomas, tried to say how the girls were as ripe and ready for eating as the fruit they were selling.'

'I did?'

'Only it wasn't an easy thing to say in French and the smiles disappeared, it made them frown.'

'Then we said we would like to buy some cherries and cider from them and that made things better, and there was a good deal of laughter about our accents and poor French. Then you asked them whether they would like to come with us for a walk and to teach us French. There was this pause, as they asked permission from their mothers. Do you remember the way the mothers examined us, there seemed to be a long pause before they finally agreed to let their daughters accompany us. But what risk was there with two monks; we were protected you see by our celibacy.'

'Our celibacy, yes. Only, they didn't know we hadn't yet taken final vows.'

Bishop Thomas was smiling.

'So, what happened next?'

'You know what happened next, Bishop Thomas.'

'I remember, they took off their aprons, kissed their mothers and walked away with us out beyond the town walls into the countryside. And there was this feeling of freedom, like a special thing had happened. I don't ever remember feeling quite like that again.' He nodded to himself. 'But I'm interrupting you Gilbert, continue.'

'We were looking for somewhere to eat the cherries and drink the cider. Somewhere hidden away where we couldn't be seen.'

'And we found somewhere.'

'Yes, a field with long grass and high walls and we sat with our backs to the stone wall next to the road, hidden from view and drank the cider and ate the cherries. They taught us bad words in French which, when we tried to say them, made them giggle.'

'They were tempting us, tempting young monks, leading us to do things we shouldn't do.' He was laughing, a loud, generous laugh that Prior Gilbert remembered.

'Yes, Thomas and then we lay down in the long grass.'

'And had our pleasure.'

They sat in silence a long moment. Gilbert remembering how Sophie had sat up and looked at him curiously, then put her arms around him and kissed him, noticing as she did so, the bracelet she was wearing, saw now, all these years later, the green stones set out on a thin metal band around her narrow wrist. He wondered what had happened to her and felt a terrible longing to be young again, sitting in a field of long grass with this pretty girl, one distant Normandy afternoon.

'Why, Prior Gilbert, do we keep these fanciful memories, what purpose do they serve?'

Prior Gilbert thought this over a moment before answering.

'I think Bishop Thomas we keep them as reminders of something that has disappeared, to which we are unable to return. They have importance because they happened to us, are part of our experience helping us to be who we are. So, a memory comes to us, often unbidden which we unwrap, examine, polish a little, telling the story to ourselves or perhaps to a friend who shared the occasion.'

He finished his wine imagining still, the field with Sophie, recalling how they had lain back on the long grass and watched the small fluffy white clouds drifting slowly across the blue sky. And the girl had said: 'Des nuages blanches dans le ciel bleu,' which she had made him repeat, a phrase like poetry that Gilbert had never forgotten. He must have said the French phrase out loud now because the Lord Bishop decided to move away from memories.

'Now Prior Gilbert' – there was an abrupt change of tone.

'A consideration of the affairs of the monastery at Holy Island please.' He had got up from the armchair and now went across to the table, picking up a document which must concern Holy Island, the most recent report on conditions there.

Prior Gilbert joined him standing in front of the table.

'We are suffering Lord Bishop, not the monastery itself you understand, we are well provisioned, but the surrounding chapels. Years of bad weather and terrible harvests have made it impossible to pay the tithes, as you will know. The people do not have enough to eat and I fear that the coming pestilence will lead to the deaths of many, those already weakened through disease and malnutrition. This will mean further years when the tithes will not be paid.'

Prior Gilbert waited but Bishop Thomas was watching him but made no comment.

'It would be good Lord Bishop if we could halt the Scots raids on our villages. They come and take the cattle and horses, kidnap for ransom, kill and set fire to dwellings...' – he paused before adding with less confidence – '...if something could be done to prevent this?'

'No, the only way to end the raids is for an English Army to march here, which is not going to happen. A campaign in France where the weather is better, the terrain more hospitable and the rewards from plunder and ransom considerably higher, means his gracious majesty Edward III will not be tempted to do battle in Scotland where poor weather,

87

mountains, few rewards and a ferocious enemy is capable of inflicting defeat.'

He shook his head.

'Unless of course, the Scotch King decides to bring an army across the border into England and then there would be a reaction; an unlikely situation but one that would devoutly to be wished.'

Prior Gilbert did not share the bishop's wish to see this happen, imagining the destruction fighting would bring the further campaigns of retaliation.

'And before you ask, I have not at Norham Castle the means to patrol the border, only a limited garrison and no money to increase the numbers.'

He finished his goblet of wine and made it clear the meeting was at an end, perhaps prompted by Prior Gilbert's request, leading him to the door which he opened for him but pausing here, pointed a finger at him.

'Prior Gilbert, I need to warn you. Brother William who you encountered as you came here, wants to be Prior of Holy Island, sees himself in your place. He has heard you have a girl in your monastery and this concerns him greatly. Brother William wants to take over from you because he believes you are old and weak allowing the communities not to pay their tithes and, in this way, risking the survival of the monastery on Holy Island.'

Prior Gilbert raised a hand to interject but was ignored as the bishop continued, 'Now this is not something that is going to happen be assured. Certainly not for a further two years or so but I may then be pressured into giving in to his request. Unless, of course, I have the opportunity to rid myself of him. Rumours of the particular form of his "celibacy" have come to me and should I find any evidence for his predilection for young boy monks, I will take immediate action and he will be unceremoniously returned to Lincoln.

I have a letter for you to take to be read out to your monks concerning their reported lack of respect for you and your position as prior.'

The bishop went back to the table returning with the missive concerned, which he handed to Prior Gilbert who received it with concern for the message which would be written there. He dreaded having to read the letter to the assembled monks with its revelation of his lack of discipline in the handling of their affairs.

Gilbert walked back down the long corridor reflecting on how a meeting which had begun in the savouring of old memories and good burgundy had been clouded over with news which he knew would lead to worry and sleepless nights in his life as prior, a position already fraught with many difficulties.

Chapter Eleven

Coming to the end of the causeway on their twice weekly journey to the monastery, Marjorie now riding the donkey as Isolde walked, they could see someone racing along the path towards them.

Isolde watched the approaching figure wondering why he should come down from the monastery to meet them. They were often together now, the only children at the monastery and she had heard several times about Alan's defeat of the bandits on the road to Durham, an account that provided every detail of the incident.

Alan was out of breath as he caught up with them, they let Marjorie ride on ahead.

'Isolde, now we are friends.'

She wasn't sure this had happened but as she thought about it, she did like him.

'I think we should do something together.'

She looked at him, wondering what this could involve.

'What being a friend means, is doing things together, you said this Isolde.'

She wasn't sure she actually had but he was continuing.

'I want to go on an adventure and go with you, go together.'

'Go where?'

Here Alan stopped and pointed to the most significant natural feature on Holy Island, the rocky crag beyond the monastery.

'Go there, climb up this mountain.'

'I don't think it is a mountain, just rocks.'

'Well, climb up the rocks.'

Isolde didn't think this sounded like a good idea and hadn't someone said it was dangerous and they shouldn't go there.

'From the top you could look out onto all the sea, Bamburgh Castle.' And seeing her continued hesitation…'You see it's where the blessed Saint Cuthbert would have gone to pray.'

This was clever, the way to give an adventure religious purpose, the way to persuade her to come.

Isolde slowly nodded.

'Alright, when do we go?'

After the morning lessons, they left the classroom, Alan moving on ahead, Isolde following thinking friends should stay together.

As they were walking beside the monastery gardens, Isolde said:

'Alan, can I show you my garden?'

She led him to a section of the vegetable area to a small separate patch with a few lettuces, onions and some ragged flowers that had finished flowering.

'This is my garden; I made this with Brother Andrew's help.'

She pointed to the rows of vegetables.

Alan had never considered gardens and didn't know what to say, found he didn't have the words and so, said what Brother Gregory did when he looked at your work.

'Very good, Isolde.'

'That's what Brother Gregory says.'

'Yes, well it is very good.'

'The bad thing' – and here she crouched down noticing where birds had eaten some of the lettuce leaves – 'the birds come and eat my lettuce.'

Then, Alan said with sudden inspiration: 'I could make a scare crow.'

She looked up at him and gave a big smile.

'Yes, a scare crow' – and he did an adult sweep of the hand to indicate the plants – 'to protect your lettuce.'

As they walked out of the monastery grounds and went along the sandy path towards the rocky crag ahead of them, Alan thought about how girls could do this, make you feel good and he did feel good, turned around now to look at the young girl following him.

At the bottom of the crag, she caught up with him and they looked at the pathway that led up to the top of the rocks. There was a pause as they realised it was not going to be easy.

Alan turned to her:

'Steep but we can do this, follow me.' And he led the way up the narrow path.

They climbed for about ten minutes, and then stopped to catch their breath. Alan looked down at her bare feet, noticing them for the first time.

'You don't have shoes?'

She was embarrassed looking down at her feet then at the new boots he was wearing. She shook her head. 'My father says my feet grow too quickly, he would have to make a new pair every week,' and then 'I don't need shoes.' She tossed back her long hair and walked quickly up the path ahead of him to make this point, thinking she really would like a pair of shoes, wooden clogs like some girls had but they couldn't afford to buy any and her father Michael the priest wasn't good at making things.

The path became steeper as they climbed on and seemed in places to disappear, the mass of rocks loomed above them like a threat, a reminder of the danger, how a slip could mean falling over the edge. Isolde didn't want to think about this but said a quick prayer and noticed how Alan was now going more slowly, taking care, using his hands for extra support.

'Here give me your hand.' And he lent down and pulled her up over a ridge of rock, helping her when she needed support, she was a girl and younger than him. Perhaps this wasn't a good idea, climbing the crag but he didn't say this to Isolde.

Then, some pebbles gave way and Isolde fell back dangerously close to the edge of the cliff, only just saving herself from disappearing over the edge. She had hurt her knee and found a piece of cloth in her pocket which she wrapped around the wound. They sat down and looked at one another.

She wanted to ask Alan whether they should go back, but didn't say the words.

They looked down the path they had just climbed, the descent looked to be more challenging.

Then, as though she had actually asked the question, he responded, 'No, we go on, we want to see what Saint Cuthbert would have seen. That's why we've come isn't it?'

It took them a further 15 minutes to reach the top with frequent halts, needing in places to go on all fours to scramble over the final sections of rock.

They sat at the top of the crag, looking at the view but the weather was changing, a storm coming in from the sea, so that the castle at Bamburgh disappeared in the mist, it began to rain heavily.

'We need a better way to go down.' Alan disappeared leaving Isolde on her own wishing she was safely at home in front of a warm fire.

'Better over here.' And he led her to a path on the opposite side of the crag.

Getting wet, the rocks now slippery, they made their way carefully down the path until they were back on the ground. Realising they were very late for their lessons they ran all the way back to the monastery.

As they got closer, they could see Brother Gregory and Marjorie waiting for them.

Alan and Isolde waited outside Prior Gilbert's door where they had been sent to be punished. They were both wet from the rain and Isolde was shivering whether from fear or the cold, she wasn't sure.

Alan turned to her. 'You don't need to worry, Prior Gilbert is a kind man and if you say to him you should be beaten, he will just give you a special task to do instead.'

They were told to enter and stood there in front of the prior's table. Prior Gilbert they could see was very angry, talking about how dangerous it was to climb the crag and how they might have been killed or seriously injured.

Then Alan said:

'Prior Gilbert, we went because we wanted to see where the blessed Saint Cuthbert would have gone to pray, only it was raining and the mist came down so we couldn't see.'

There was no response to this which disappointed him. So he tried what had worked before.

'I think you should beat us, what we did was bad, very bad and could have led to death or injury.'

He wasn't sure as he said this whether you could beat girls, looking at Isolde next to him, standing there with her long hair, her bare feet on the wooden floor of the prior's parlour which he could see had suffered some cuts on the journey up the crag thinking how different girls were, how they looked, how they behaved. He didn't really understand his friend.

'But I don't think you should beat Isolde, it was my idea.'

Prior Gilbert took out from the cupboard behind him a stick as they watched and Isolde who had never received a beating of any kind, wondered how painful it could be, a series of blows delivered on the hand.

'Alan, come here, put out your hand.'

The prior held the hand in place, so he could be sure Alan did not withdraw it and then brought the stick down with force onto the hand. The blow was delivered four times. Isolde could see the bloody marks on his hand, wondering again how much it must hurt but he didn't cry out, there was just a sharp intake of breath at each blow.

Alan stepped back and she could see him look down at his hand and then clench and unclench it.

Isolde came forward and put out her hand.

'No, Isolde, I'm not going to beat you. This is not a place where we beat girls and Alan, as he said, suggested this unhappy and dangerous activity.'

She came back to where Alan was standing.

'I need to tell both of you that I have – despite this afternoon's action – been very pleased with the progress you have been making here at the monastery. However, as you may know your lessons will now be ended as from next week the monastery will be closed and you will have to return home. The pestilence is coming and we need to ensure the monastery is not affected by illness.

There will just be the penitential procession when I will lead the people of Lowyk down here to the priory church. And so today's dangerous exploit will be the last you will be able to get up to for many months. But hopefully, we will see you back at your lessons, sometime in the future.'

Chapter Twelve

Prior Gilbert stood outside Lowick Chapel ready to lead the penitential Procession to the monastery at Holy Island. Beside him was Brother Andrew with the large cross from the chapel which legend pretended had been the one the blessed Saint Cuthbert used as he converted the pagans in this district, planting this same cross in each village and telling of the Lord Jesus Christ. A good story but not one the prior could give credence to, and yet, looking at the wooden cross Brother Andrew was holding now, worn and certainly old, it could just have survived as a venerated link to Saint Cuthbert, hidden away during the Viking raids and other times of conflict. Who was he to call into dispute what people chose to believe?

It seemed a long wait before the procession could begin, and his attention now was drawn to the chapel, the damaged stone work and thatched roof; like a poor person's ragged garment, he thought, with the holes failing to conceal the emaciated body within, the building was in much need of repair. He noticed for the first time the tympanum above the chapel door made of red stone with a strange pattern of lines and circles and wondered how this helped protect the building, ensuring any evil was left outside.

Brother Andrew said quietly, 'This is a poor place, Prior.'

Prior Gilbert watched the women gathering for the procession as the men stood around in small groups, talking in low voices as though they hadn't yet decided to join. You could tell immediately that this was a poor place, they would have worn their best clothing for the procession to Holy Island, yet none of them had anything special to wear. A battered community but one, Prior Gilbert thought, which was still proud, defiant in the face of years of adversity.

'This Lowyk is a proud place damaged by war and pestilence, Brother Andrew, failed harvests and Scots raids. They have nothing, they don't have enough to eat and yet they are supposed to pay us annual tithes of corn and beans, peas and then, the lamb tithes.'

The priest of Lowyk , Father Michael joined them with Isolde who greeted Prior Gilbert and Brother Andrew, with a smile which quickly disappeared, like a person at a funeral, nervous of showing pleasure at a time of death.

Prior Gilbert had wondered whether Isolde should be given a special role in the procession, aware that Brother William would be leading the other group from Ancroft to Holy Island but decided he was not going to be influenced by the man who wanted to succeed him.

'Isolde, I would like you to carry the incense.' And he produced from his cloak the smallest sensor the monastery possessed.

She looked pleased, joining her father at the front of the procession, as the men finally moved into place followed by the women and children and two carts pulled by mules for the elderly and most frail.

Prior Gilbert turned and faced the community before him. There were special prayers to be said on these occasions but he wanted to say just a few plain words, the formal prayers in Latin carried no meaning for them, merely sounds which while providing familiar comfort for some, failed to communicate any message.

'Lord God Almighty, look down on us with mercy as we make this penitential procession, asking for your protection for ourselves, our families and all in the village of Lowyk during this fearful time as we await the approach of the pestilence.'

There was a murmured "Amen".

He then turned back to face east the direction they would be walking, waiting a moment for silence, for the nervous shuffling to cease, before starting the procession and leading the people away from their village.

There was coughing and the sound of a baby crying and then, a special quiet descended as they moved forward, a hundred souls walking down past the wooden dwellings of Lowyk before turning left down the Devil's Causeway the Roman Road that would take them towards Holy Island and the monastery.

Prior Gilbert had never before led his parishioners down to the priory church on Holy Island. The words from Saint Matthew's Gospel came to him: 'Harassed and helpless like sheep without a shepherd,' wasn't he the shepherd leading his flock, the familiar Bible image, realised here, now, in these extraordinary circumstances? It humbled him to have such heavy responsibility.

He didn't want to turn and look at the crowd stretching out behind him, in case it might diminish the potency of the occasion, feeling that everything had to be done in a certain way for this public demonstration of penance to be acceptable.

He couldn't therefore actually see those following him but felt their presence as something tangible and immense, the lives of all those in the village coming together at this moment in one body to ask for protection and forgiveness.

The strips of cultivated land stretching down away from the road were empty of the men and animals who would labour here, as though this was a Sunday; beyond the parish boundaries the line of the cold, grey sea marked the horizon. There was no wind, only a curious stillness as though the landscape, the trees and fields and hills were watching their progress, observing this strange behaviour that had brought a community together to atone for their sins.

And then unexpectedly there was a murmur from the ranks of those behind him. Sounding first, like a single moan from one person, then gathering in strength as others took up the funeral dirge, until the whole body of those present joined, as though in anticipation of the grieving to come. Gilbert had heard this before in churchyards, from the distressed members of a bereaved family; this was different, as though the whole community shared the distress of damaged lives, now threatened with further and more extensive hurt. The keening died as it had started, reduced to a single complaining groan and then silence, as they walked on but which would be repeated at various points of the journey and later, would be what Prior Gilbert retained from this solemn procession to the monastery.

From the corner of his eye, Prior Gilbert could see Isolde, walking just behind him, looking serious, and concentrating as she swung the sensor releasing the incense which quickly dispersed into the open air. The incense would run out he thought, long before they reached the monastery but he saw that she was conserving the perfume, only using the sensor from time to time; a clever girl. Then came a thought he regretted, for the implications it contained for the dangers to her health. Would this time of pestilence provide the special occasion in which she would participate, for which she had been saved?

They came to Sam's House where a further group of parishioners were gathered, waiting to join the procession. Then, they were moving forward again down the hill by Lowick Mill and then up past Kent Stone farm towards Mount Joy where pilgrims had their first glimpse of Holy Island, hidden from Lowick by a series of low hills.

The procession stopped here for a moment to observe the low lying island with the distinctive crag, the priory church and monastery with the cluster of dwellings. This was his monastery, the place he had lived for all these years. It looked from this vantage point like a small, isolated placed dwarfed by the sky and vast surrounding sea.

Isolde was tired, they had walked for three hours and now had finally reached the crossing point to Holy Island. Three years having lessons at the monastery hadn't cured her fear of the causeway. She couldn't stop her heart racing, looking across the sands now to check, as she always did, that the sea wasn't rushing in to catch them.

What frightened her was the wild, open space between the island and mainland, there was no protection. The sands they were walking on, stretching out in every direction waiting for the sea to come to cover them again, the huge sky above. There was nowhere to hide from all these terrible forces and she shivered, remembering too well the horrors when she had been alone here in the dark, as the waters came. She said the special prayer to Saint Cuthbert, given to her by Prior Gilbert, asking the saint to protect her on this dangerous crossing. A prayer she used every time she came over here, thinking now again, to calm her, of the story of Moses crossing the Red Sea, seeing in the crowd of people following, how this was like the Israelites fleeing the Egyptians, only they weren't being pursued.

As she walked on, it came to her that today they were fleeing, trying to escape the terrors of the pestilence, the reason they were here in this procession. The thought of the disease scared her, she had heard about the black marks that came on the bodies of the sick with their message of certain death.

As they arrived on Holy Island and walked up past the long stretch of marsh and sand dunes to the monastery, the moaning began again.

In the village, there were people selling protection from the disease, stretching their hands out to the penitents offering small bottles of tonic, bundles of dried herbs, potions and calling out the benefits of their products. A few penitents stopped to look more closely, examining the products, occasionally buying something.

One old lady in rags pushed her way forward, standing directly in front of Isolde, obstructing her, stopping her walking on. The woman held out a bundle of dried herbs wrapped in a piece of old brown cloth; she spoke urgently in a husky voice.

'Take this child, to protect you, keep you safe, you don't want to die do you, you pretty young thing. I collected these herbs myself, by full moon, a special, power here, the power to protect, to keep you safe.'

There was a wild look in her eyes and her breath smelt.

Brother Andrew pushed her aside, muttering something about superstition.

They reached the door of the priory, when the keening cries faded to nothing. Prior Gilbert waited for the stragglers to catch up, the frail and lame to be supported and join them. Then with the cross held high, they processed solemnly forward into the body of his priory church, the community of Lowyk behind him. They had to push their way through the ranks of the silent, restless congregation standing there, waiting to hear the message from the Bishop of Durham. Waiting to have explained to them what they had done to deserve this fearful affliction of the pestilence and how they should repent.

Isolde made her way through the nave of the church, following Prior Gilbert, almost getting lost in the crowd but still having time to appreciate the feeling of this special building, remembering how as a small girl, half-drowned she had come here to seek refuge. This was a place she loved.

A small group of monks were standing in front of the altar. As she joined them, she could see the tall man with a pointed nose watching her, saw him turn to Brother Gregory to ask something and she could hear Brother Gregory answer: 'Isolde, daughter of the priest.' The man nodded but continued to stare at her making her feel uncomfortable, Why was he looking at her like this, what did he want? She didn't want the man to watch her, it wasn't a friendly way to look at her. Isolde, bowed her head, she didn't like the man, didn't want to be near him.

The man left the group to climb the steps up to the pulpit, Brother Gregory whispered his name to Isolde:

'Brother William from Durham.'

Brother William surveyed the large crowd gathered before him and then drew out the Lord Bishop's letter.

'You will ask yourselves, what have we done to deserve the terrible affliction of the great pestilence. I have here the letter from the Lord Bishop of Durham who has sent me here this morning specially to read out to you this missive written in his very own hand.'

And here, Brother William held up the document, turning to each side of the priory church to ensure everyone could see the document with its ribbon and the red seal of the Lord Prince Bishop of Durham.

'A missive which will explain precisely why you deserve this terrible punishment.' He began reading out the message in a slow magisterial manner.

'It is to be feared that the most likely explanation is that human sensuality – the fire that blazes up as a result of Adam's sin and which from adolescence onwards is an incitement to wrong doing – has now plumbed greater depths of evil, producing a multitude of sins which have provoked the divine anger, by a just judgement to revenge.'

He put down the document and looked at them before repeating:

'Has now plumbed greater depths of evil, producing a multitude of sins...which have provoked the divine anger, by a just judgement to revenge.'

Then came the terrible indictment that Brother William had used when addressing the priors at Durham Cathedral: those inflicted with the disease were being punished, suffering the divine wrath and therefore could not expect the comfort of paradise, slamming shut the doors of redemption with the fear of eternal damnation, burning in hell fire.

There was a pause as Brother William came down from the pulpit officiously rolling up the missive he had just read out. The crowd now turned to Prior Gilbert waiting for him to take his place in the pulpit.

Prior Gilbert waited a moment thinking about what they had all just heard and worrying about what he knew he had to do. He climbed the steps to the pulpit slowly and from this elevated position looked down on the parishioners who had been led here this morning. The priory church was full, people gathered in the nave, around the pulpit and up into the choir, every space taken by the parishioners of this Holy Island parish, his parishioners, waiting to hear further fearful denunciation on how their sinful lives had led to this divine punishment.

He saw the fear in their eyes and felt huge pity for them, here were the men and women with whom as Prior of the monastery he had shared the succession of tribulations and difficulties that had shaped their lives. He felt for them a special love.

They had already suffered here was a further affliction the most terrible of all. He wanted to provide an element of hope turning to the words of St Paul in his letter to the Romans, at a time of the saint's own suffering and imminent death.

'Hope does not disappoint.'

He repeated the phrase with greater emphasis: 'Hope does not disappoint.'

Someone shouted out from the back of the church: 'We don't hear you, Prior!'

Prior Gilbert had a small, weak voice and now with the most important message he had ever had to give, he couldn't make himself heard. He was failing, failing in perhaps his most important task as prior of Holy Island, he couldn't deliver his message, couldn't comfort those in desperate need of comfort, frightened by the coming pestilence and terrified by the implication of Brother William's words.

He raised his arms and let them drop again to indicate helplessness, his inability to be heard. Then he noticed that those closest to the pulpit were being asked what had been said by those nearest them, making them turn to repeat the words to those behind, so the message was passed on.

And then Brother Gregory was in the narrow pulpit standing beside him, saying the words for him, becoming his voice.

'Hope does not disappoint.'

The phrase was repeated again, the process of passing the message to others becoming established, as though this was the normal way to spread the words from the pulpit; creating a movement in the congregation, as people turned to pass on the message, so that the words ran down the length of the nave and around the choir, like the flow of water with the murmuring sound of this repetition filling the priory church. And with each repetition, the phrase seemed to become stronger, a more powerful antidote at this time of strife.

Prior Gilbert waited for the movement to end and silence to return before continuing, starting up the process again. Delivering the words into space, launching them into the void, where their offer of comfort and mercy could be taken up, gathered by each person present there.

'I do not believe that those who suffer from the pestilence have sinned.'

He waited for Brother Gregory to repeat this and watched as the message passed away down the massed members of his parish from Tweedmouth and Ancroft, Lowyk and Kyloe and all the smaller villages and hamlets that came to worship here.

'You must pray for salvation and the doors of paradise will be open for you.'

What had begun as an attempt to pass on the message had become something more powerful, each phrase taking on added significance, a special resonance. He was going to say more, had prepared further words but stopped here, giving prominence to his message of hope which further words were likely to dilute.

He bowed his head in prayer to thank the Almighty that he had been given a voice and then looked up in surprise there was clapping and some shouting, people were smiling again, a celebration that they were not to disappear into the eternal flames of damnation. Seeing their prior as the source of this hope, the expression of their salvation, people were shaking his hand as he came down from the pulpit and was among them again.

Prior Gilbert went back to where he had been standing next to Brother William who shook his head in anger and then forced his way through the crowd to leave the church, muttering how the message from the Lord, Prince Bishop of Durham had been ignored, deliberately obscured.

Only he wasn't able to reach the door of the church, his way blocked deliberately by members of the congregation, unhappy with the message he had given, there was some pushing and shoving and he turned an anxious and angry face to look for help. Brother Gregory went down to free him but there were further blows before he reached the safety of the monastery lawns.

Prior Gilbert watched him leave.

'I don't feel Brother William will remember the parishioners of Holy Island with any great affection.'

Chapter Thirteen

'Now, Mac, what's done to protect Lowyk?'

Mac Soult extended his legs and made himself comfortable in front of the priest's fire. His large size blocking the warmth from Marjorie and Isolde sitting behind him. Isolde noticed the holes in the boots he was wearing.

'Father Michael much has been decided,' he spoke excitedly as though the measures really would ward off the pestilence ticking them off on his fingers.

'First, watches are to be set up at each road leading to the village, manned all day and through the night so, no one from outside the village arrives here. I am to be on the night watch tonight, at the South Road. We will also, light a bonfire there to ward off the evil air on which the pestilence is born, a bonfire which will burn night and day. Anyone coming here from outside the village will be forced away, we will be armed.'

'Then' – he pointed to the second of his raised fingers – 'there will be further bonfires in the centre of the village, here by the chapel and down by the hostel tower.'

There was a pause as he looked at the third raised finger trying to remember what else there was to mention, something to do with Father Michael and the reason for his visit here.

'Using the pilgrims' hostel?'

'Oh and then…' He remembered what he had to ask: 'The reeve wants to know whether the pilgrim hostel and chapel could be used to look after the sick when their families are unable to.' There was a dramatic pause as he looked around at them his eyes wide. 'Because they've died.'

For perhaps three weeks, Lowyk waited for the arrival of the pestilence, cut off and isolated from other villages which in their turn were closed down, forcing away outsiders. Fear and rumours circulated, no one sure where they came from; always reports at third hand from someone who knew, who had actually seen or heard: of the poisoned air circulating in the country about them and numbers dying, burial pits having to be dug to bury the corpses, of a single small child who survived from an isolated dwelling found on her own, wandering the road seeking refuge after her family had all perished.

Then the disease came closer, the first cases declared at Doddington, just five miles south of Lowyk, suggesting, what had already been apparent, the disease was steadily moving north, nothing able to halt, its deadly progress. The whole village held its breath, more men were added to the night watches to be certain no refugees from Doddington tried to get into Lowyk bringing the suffering with them. A state of heightened vigilance prevailed, people keeping away from others, in case the disease had already arrived unbeknown, was at this very moment circulating among them.

Then came reports of pestilence from Ancroft to the north. People gathered to consider this information, if the disease had been at Doddington now Ancroft, then Lowyk lying between these two places had maybe missed the affliction.

110

And as further reports to the north arrived, that Berwick was suffering and places on the coast, the village dared to believe that it had been spared.

They waited a few more days and still no cases reported and so, people slowly began to relax, like those who discard winter clothing with the coming of warmer weather, though aware that further cold might still come, maybe this was the hope of which Prior Gilbert had spoken.

'Is no sign of pestilence then, John. Ancroft has it and Doddington but not here.'

'Happens we're good people here, not like those Ancroft folk.'

'You think we going to be safe then?'

'Aye, will come to nought.'

'Ye better be right, John, I've ploughing to finish.'

'Nay to worry, man!' And old John who had seen it all before, moved away slowly on down the street, nodding to himself, convinced of how things would be.

Belief slowly turned to conviction; if the disease was going to come it would have arrived already. Some, perhaps even believing, that they did indeed lead good lives or perhaps, if honest, that the village had already suffered the wrath of God over many years and perhaps the Lord had now, chosen to show mercy to this wretched place. Others felt that the penitential procession had delivered them, protected them from the suffering.

The night watch became just a token protection with only a couple of men in place at each of the entry points to the village, the two bonfires reduced to a single fire.

With the monastery closed, Isolde was looking after some of the small children in the village. Walking back up towards the chapel, she heard excited voices and saw a group gathered by the bonfire. A man, she didn't know very well a newcomer to the village, was telling the growing crowd about something he had just seen. Isolde made her way forward to listen.

'Telling you, I saw them with me own eyes, rats, an army of rats, black rats, hundreds of 'em, heading this way, heading for Lowyk.'

'How far?' The authoritative voice of Gilbert Duff, village reeve.

'About three miles south, coming down the fields by the Devil's Causeway.'

'Coming from Doddington then,' someone said.

There was silence. Isolde noticed the way people looked away refusing to meet the eyes of others, turning in to their own thoughts, they were frightened.

The reeve spoke:

'Soon be dark, have to surprise and destroy them, every one of them. We need to find where they settle for the night and then go out there and kill them. Stop them reaching our lands, stop them entering Lowyk.

William Gretwood, William Gunson, ride out now, find the rats, do not disturb them, they will gather for the night in a ditch or beside a burn where they have water and food to gather. Then one of you stays watching, and the other ride back to report, taking us to where they are gathered. We need every man, dividing into two groups one with lighted torches to drive the rats into the open where the second group will be lying in wait for them and we will then' – he looked around at the men gathered there – 'club them to death.'

There were murmurs of agreement.

The words frightened Isolde, what made the rats dangerous, the need to have them destroyed? She watched the men leaving to carry out their task.

'Gwen, what makes rats dangerous. I don't understand?'

The woman turned and looked at her, surprised she didn't know.

'The rats is a sign see, Isolde, that the pestilence is coming, they don't bring the pestilence but come with the bad air, like they know there's going to be death. Killing the rats might help but don't think will stop the dying, the pestilence's come,' she was sobbing as she turned away.

The village was in a state of frenzy, the news spreading fast in the small community, everyone gathering by the chapel to watch as the men gathered with clubs and torches, the torches unlit until they attacked the rats.

Many of the women waited out by the chapel wall for their men to return to know what had happened, how the black rats had been destroyed. It was like this when a raiding party left to cross the border, the importance of knowing whether there was grieving or celebration to be done.

The men returned some hours later, small silent groups, exhausted, injured. Some sinking to the ground others, standing confused, their clothes torn and their arms, faces and legs smeared with blood, their own and those of the rats they had slaughtered, shaking their heads at the enormity of the experience. The women waiting there led them away.

There were confused accounts. The ambush hadn't worked. As they had raced to attack the rats at the edge of the field, they had stumbled on a much larger body lying there in the dark which, as they were disturbed turned to attack, launching themselves on the men. The vicious struggle that ensued revealed only by the flickering light of torches which had to be dropped, as the men, needing to defend themselves, fought back, tearing from them the biting, scratching animals, trying at the same time to batter them with their clubs. Men shouting and swearing, trying to make themselves heard, above the terrible squealing of thousands of rats.

One man, his clothes in shreds, stood there by the chapel, trembling, wide eyed a look of terror on this face, unable to speak, to find answers to the questions of the crowd that now gathered around him, those wanting to hear more, fascinated by this horrific event which seemed a portent of the agonies to come. Then, words came rushing, a torrent of phrases but like the chaos of the event, they made no sense.

'Young John Little, has anyone seen him?'

They turned from the man who stumbled away, to see Gilbert Duff, reeve, leader of the raid.

'He hasn't returned.'

They rode out to find him, the reeve and two others, returning at first light with a covered figure slumped across the back of a mule that they led away, not wanting to reveal the injuries that killed the young man. They never spoke of the terrors of the search to find the lifeless body.

Three days later, the first deaths from the pestilence came to the village of Lowick, four of the men who had been in the group that had attacked the rats.

Chapter Fourteen

Epistle One

To Gilbert, Prior of the monastery at Holy Island

I, Brother Andrew, am pleased to provide you with this first account from the village of Lowyk where through the Grace of God, you have sent me to serve during this time of pestilence.

Prior, the numbers who suffer grow daily and there are few families spared.

The pilgrim hostel is now a place for the afflicted, particularly orphaned children and others for whom there is no care. Here we can provide food and shelter, give them comfort through the words of our Lord Jesus Christ.

The lady Marjorie and Isolde, daughter of the priest help me here, attending to the needs of those who can no longer help themselves, watching through the night with those who pass the final hours of their time here in this world of pain and sufferance before attaining the promise of eternal life – believing with you Prior Gilbert that the gates of heaven can be pushed open for those innocents who suffer.

Food has become scarce, supplies of flour exhausted and so with others I visited the mill at Lowick to discover the building locked, the mill abandoned, for the miller and his family have fled from contact with the pestilence. Forcing open the door to the mill, a search revealed a secret vault containing six bags of flour which we acquired.

It has proved possible to use the outside oven of the hostel to bake bread – prepared by the good lady Marjorie – and in this way have provided for the needs of the village, a blessing indeed and an answer to our earnest prayers to the Blessed Saint Cuthbert for this gift of our daily bread – limiting each family to one loaf.

Prior Gilbert, please pray for us here in this hour of our desperate need.

Your Brother in Christ,
Andrew.
Post scriptum: If in your goodness, Prior Gilbert, you were able to deliver provisions from the monastery to us here in Lowyk, these I assure you would be most graciously received.

Dividing the work each of them had to do, Brother Andrew decided that he would be with the men on the lower floor of the hostel with Marjorie caring for the sick women on the upper floor and Isolde using the small chapel on the same floor for the children who came to them.

No sooner had this decision been made and the hostel opened, than a steady stream of the sick and dying arrived. There was no time to consider the terrible risk she was taking, no time even to pray for her own safety, there was immediate work to be done as the frightened children, many having already seen their mothers and fathers die in front of them, were brought to her. You didn't need to check for the marks of the disease, there was about each small victim, evidence of coming death betrayed by the terrible odour coming from their bodies.

You remember beginnings, the first child, a small boy, was carried into the chapel and laid down on the straw that had been placed there. The boy was crying out for his mother and Isolde had a moment of terror because she didn't know what she should do, how to stop the trembling, to comfort this dying child. She knelt down beside the small person who had stopped calling for his mother and was watching her, waiting for her to do something. For a moment, she was afraid to touch the diseased form lying in front of her, noticing the sweat soaked blond hair, the blue eyes from which life seemed already to be fading.

There was at that moment the sound of a commotion downstairs, a man shouting out and swearing, struggling and the calm voice of Brother Andrew, talking to him quietly.

Isolde then knew what she had to do, she smiled at the anxious face and put forward her arms using her hands to touch the diseased body, feeling as she did so that her fingers could soothe and comfort. Holding him so the shivering ended, the anxiety reduced.

'What's your name?'

'Henry, Isolde.' And he smiled a wan distant smile that seemed to take the very life out of him, for the eyes now closed and with a little shiver, the boy was still.

She held onto the now lifeless form feeling the warmth slowly leave the little body and cried.

Someone called, and she turned to see two small children, a boy and girl standing at the top of the stairs holding hands, needing her.

She brought the two children into the chapel and the boy said pointing to the figure she had just left lying on the straw.

'Is he dead?'

Isolde nodded. 'He is called Henry.'

'I know, Isolde, he's my friend.'

And she realised that things had to move on. These two were not sick but needed to be looked after must have been brought here as orphans and had to be separated from those afflicted, taken away from the agony of the dying.

There was a small vestry next to the chapel with a table, crucifix on the wall and she brought the two of them here and sat them down.

'Are you hungry?'

They were and she wondered how many days had passed since they had had something to eat, as she went to find something for them.

As the days became weeks, the pestilence raged through the village like a hungry predator, nothing able to stop its constant ravages, taking young and old at random, the strong as well as the weak, men, women and children. The survivors not daring to believe they would be spared but merely waiting for the time they too would be afflicted, experiencing the marks on their bodies, the period of fever before death and the common grave.

You don't get used to children dying but accept the reality of the world around you. For Isolde, it was as though she had entered a different space where the sick and usually dying children took up her time. Learning how to talk to them and comfort them, providing the words and using her hands to calm the frenzy which often took hold of them, never leaving them alone in this time of greatest need in their short lives.

Isolde overheard people talking about her. How she was able to reassure children agitated and disturbed on their arrival at the hostel, so that they left this life at peace. This was something that first pleased her but then, she didn't really want. Didn't want to hear or answer questions about it, needing just to be left alone, able to do what she was doing. She was too tired to reflect very much on what she did, the effect she was having but fiercely didn't want to be different.

Marjorie and Brother Andrew noticed how those arriving at the hostel would ask for Isolde by name, wanting her to be with them often calling for her in their final agony, as though she might save them. Although this was not mentioned, people remembered how she had somehow survived the ocean and how there was a belief at the time there would be some special purpose for this salvation.

'Brother Andrew, I want to talk with you about Isolde.'

They moved outside a moment next to where the day's bread was being baked. It was Marjorie who spoke first.

'You've heard what people are saying Brother Andrew. The belief has returned that Isolde has' – she shrugged – 'special powers, is able not just to comfort but perhaps also, to heal.'

'I don't think Isolde believes this.'

Marjorie shook her head. 'She just wants to be treated as normal an ordinary girl, helping out in this time of great need.' She paused before adding: 'She has certainly a gift.'

Brother Andrew considered for a long time without replying, there was about this a great difficulty, one he would need to consult about with Prior Gilbert.

'I think until the word is spoken we should not be worried.'

'You mean miracle.'

'Yes.' He didn't repeat the word as though afraid of the power it contained, and how it might lead to the disruption of their current lives with its expectation of healing.

Epistle Two

To Gilbert, Prior of the monastery at Holy Island

I, Brother Andrew, am pleased to provide you with this further account from the village of Lowyk where through the Grace of God, you have sent me to serve during this time of pestilence.

Prior Gilbert, the situation here is worsening as more become afflicted by the pestilence. We are lucky to have the pilgrims' hostel as a place to treat the sick and are very grateful to you for the provisions you have, in your great mercy, provided for us.

I would like to make you aware of the devotion of my fellow helpers at the hostel, Marjorie and Isolde who work tirelessly to support and comfort and care for the many we are treating, most of whom do not survive their affliction.

It is about Isolde that I would like to seek your advice as this is someone you know, of her previous life and circumstances. Marjorie has shared with me her concerns which I confirm.

Isolde has a special ability to calm those in distress who approach the end of their lives. This is talked about throughout the ville de Lowyk. People are remembering that she is someone special who survived the terrible experience of being nearly lost to the incoming tide. At the time, I believe there was a consideration of whether this salvation could be a miracle but that in the absence of any witness something that could not be proved.

Our problem here Prior Gilbert is that many of the afflicted call out for her by name and are beginning to see her as a source of healing. Isolde herself, does not want to be special but there is this danger where special healing is seen to take place through her intervention I would like advice on how I should proceed in these difficult circumstances.

Isolde is still young and despite her determination and faith, the work she is doing makes her vulnerable and were people to pressure her, asking to be healed, I fear very much that she would no longer be able to continue in her role at the hostel.

Prior Gilbert, please continue to pray for us here in this hour of our desperate need.

Your Brother in Christ,
Andrew.

Post scriptum: If in your goodness Prior Gilbert you were able to continue the supply of provisions from the monastery to us here in the ville de Lowyk, these I assure you would be most gratefully received.

Prior Gilbert read the missive, before putting it back on his table, picked it up again to read for a second time. Then walked to the window and looked out at the grey sea.

Isolde looked up to see the small girl being brought to her, the man laid her carefully down on the straw and there was a groan from the still form. The man shook his head to indicate that here was another child who would be dying.

Isolde took a deep breath and walked towards the place where the child lay. The small girl had her eyes closed and for a moment, Isolde thought she had already died. She crouched down beside the body and touched the girl on the shoulder expecting no reaction but the small girl opened her eyes, gave a weak smile at Isolde, before closing them again.

There came over Isolde at this moment a feeling she would describe to herself later as one of confidence, the certainty that she could help the child, save her that this was why she had been spared from the sea all those years ago. Everything that had happened to her seemed to be a preparation for this moment.

She now took both the small, cold hands in hers and started to pray.

Marjorie looking for Isolde had found her in the middle of the night, the single burning candle revealing the kneeling form of the girl, still holding the child's hands. This was not something that had happened before and although Marjorie spoke softly to Isolde there was no response, she was deeply engaged in an impossible healing process. She walked away realising what was happening and troubled by what she saw.

Isolde woke when it was morning, the sun lighting up the small chapel, coming around as though from a deep sleep, for a moment not knowing where she was or what she had been doing but feeling completely exhausted as though all the strength had gone out of her. She realised she was not holding the small hands; the little girl was no longer lying on the straw beside her.

She knew what that meant, the girl had died, had been taken away to be buried, they hadn't wanted to wake and tell her.

Isolde walked slowly out of the chapel, telling herself to remember, she had no special ability. Had she really thought the child could be saved?

Marjorie appeared looking worried.

'The girl died then.' And Isolde shrugged, trying not to show her deep disappointment, telling herself this is was what was happening there was nothing anyone could do to halt this.

'Isolde, I need to talk to you.' She opened her arms to the girl she had helped bring up; the closest Isolde had ever had to a mother.

Marjorie whispered the words as she held her, 'The girl is alive, it seems there has been a complete recovery, no one understands, they are saying there has been a miracle.'

Epistle Three

To Gilbert, Prior of the monastery at Holy Island

I, Brother Andrew, am pleased to provide you with this further account from the village of Lowyk where through the Grace of God, you have sent me to serve during this time of pestilence.

I'm afraid to be the bearer of bad news in the midst of all the further troubles with which the ville de Lowyk is

afflicted during this time of pestilence. The girl Isolde, daughter of the priest who is well known to us from her time here at the monastery has become ill. This is not the pestilence. She is however, in a state of collapse and needs to be taken from here in order to recover for I fear otherwise she will prove to be a further victim of the awful times in which we are living. She is not responding in any way to our ministrations and lies without moving, unable to speak or communicate.

What we were affeered would happen has taken place. A small girl who was dying has been saved through the ministrations of Isolde who prayed with the sick child through the night. In the morning, there was a complete recovery, the child was cured of the pestilence! I Brother Andrew, saw this with my own eyes. Here in the ville de Lowyk they are saying there has been a miracle, the girl's mother telling everyone what has happened and how her child has been saved and that Isolde made this happen.

I'm not sure Isolde believed this but then, already exhausted, tired out through the work she has been doing, she found every sick person wanting to be cured by her, angry when this failed to happen. As the days passed, it became more difficult for her and Isolde began to suffer until she came to be in the state in which she now finds herself, closed off from the world around her, something I Brother Andrew have never seen before.

I am of the belief that Isolde needs a time of complete rest at the monastery if she is going to recover and should be carried back on the cart that will be bringing provisions to us here at Lowyk today.

Prior Gilbert, I know you will continue to pray for us here in this hour of our desperate need.

Your Brother in Christ,
Andrew.

Chapter Fifteen

Prior Gilbert looked at Isolde, sitting across the refectory table from him. She had slept for three days and only now had the strength to move from her room and take refreshment. She looked pale and exhausted with dark rings under her eyes and there was something missing. It took him a moment to realise, there was no spirit left, as though this had been emptied from her, here was no longer the Isolde he had known.

'I remember Isolde, a small girl sitting where you are now eating bread and honey.'

She looks up at him but there is no smile, just a pause watching him a moment before continuing to eat. Gilbert feels this terrible sense of loss for the small child, saved from the sea, remembering how she had looked down at her small hands as she tried to find the words to describe what had happened to her, how she had been saved. The small child has gone forever, he thought and now has become this damaged, hurt person in front of him and he was to blame, this was his fault.

He stood up, put a hand on her shoulder, then left to go to matins, the service he had been going to ask her to attend. This was going to take a long time and apart from praying for her, he didn't know what he could do to help, how they would be able to communicate again, perhaps this wasn't going to happen.

Prior Gilbert came to a halt in the middle of the corridor, berating himself for not retaining the sense of hope essential in these terrible times. reminding himself that Isolde was better, now able to leave the security of her room, she was sick it was true but still living, she hadn't succumbed to the terrible pestilence.

And he would talk to her, try to make her understand what had happened, going all the way back to the initial incident on the causeway. He would need to prepare carefully these meetings, make sure he understood himself what all of this was about, and make her understand that it was his actions that were to blame that he alone had brought all this on her.

He would arrange to see her every day, bring her books to read from his library, arrange for special food to be prepared for her to give her strength and allow her to fully recover.

Prior Gilbert walked on towards the priory church appreciating the sunshine as he came out into the open, pausing a moment before entering the magnificent building and leading the service. He was convinced the real Isolde would return and he would hear again her laughter.

In the absence of any pilgrims or visitors, the monastery had almost ceased to exist as a working establishment, Brother Gregory had been sent to Ancroft, Brother Andrew to Lowyk and most of the younger monks had returned to Durham at their request, for there was little for them to do. Only the kitchen staff and some of the older monks remained to look after the animals and keep the gardens functioning, their work becoming more important now that they were providing cartloads of provisions to send up to the afflicted villages.

Isolde found she was unable to read or do any writing, unable to concentrate on any task. She had to be moving, walking around the monastery and grounds, following each day a chosen circuit.

One morning, news came that Brother Andrew had fallen sick with the pestilence and wasn't expected to recover.

They brought his body back to the monastery for burial and Isolde attended the service in the priory church, and then followed the coffin out in the rain to where he was to be buried. There was only a small group of mourners to gather in the churchyard as she watched her friend's coffin being lowered into the ground didn't feel grief, just a numbness, there had been too many deaths. Looking at the monastery buildings around her she realised she wanted to be away from here, leave the monastery, this was something she had done and with which she was now finished. She needed to move somewhere different, somewhere beyond the line of sea invisible this morning which framed the horizon of her life here.

The weather begins to improve; there are cold days and bright sunshine. Isolde starts to walk further afield finding on the far side of the island vast empty beaches where she can be alone. Here she can disappear into herself, walking for hours, turning to see her footprints in the sand stretching far behind her into the distance, surprised to see how far she has come. She would then sit on the sand and watch the sea's constant movement, the seagulls drifting in the blue sky; before getting up and moving on again, trying to keep her mind blank to drive away the questions that kept coming, the images of dying children, she hasn't been able to save.

For days she walks on her own, like this seeing no one. Then, one morning a distant figure appears coming across the sands towards her. Isolde changes direction to avoid them, not wishing a meeting, not wanting to talk to anyone, annoyed by this interruption but the figure continues to come closer changing direction to match her own.

Then she hears her name. The person is now right by her, she forces herself to look up, seeing a tall man she doesn't recognise, the sun is in her eyes and so she prepares to walk on but he speaks.

'Isolde, you don't know me?'

Then, before she realises what she is doing, she has thrown her arms around him, holding him tight like a drowning person finding unexpected support.

They walk together back to the monastery. Alan telling her everything about his life at Norham Castle as a page: the skirmishes with the Scots, how he had learnt to play the lute and would sing for her ladyship in her chamber.

After a moment, their hands join, like brother and sister she thinks, enjoying the warmth of his touch. It seems natural but she knows this is a moment she will always remember, walking with him across the sands.

When he asked about her, what it had been like at Lowyk during the pestilence, she shook her head, wouldn't answer not wanting to talk about what she had endured.

When Alan has gone again, she misses him terribly, reliving every moment of the short visit, how before leaving he had turned and looked at her a long moment embarrassing her by the intensity of his gaze, before saying how beautiful she now was and kissing her hand.

Then leaving to ride back to Norham Castle, back to the world of chivalry with which he was now engaged of knights and their ladies, a world she would never be able to enter.

Chapter Sixteen

Isolde had difficulty sleeping and waking in the middle of the night unable to go back to sleep, remembered how Prior Gilbert had said she should come to talk to him that he often worked through the night, something Alan had already told her.

She saw the light under his door and stood outside a moment before knocking. The door was opened Prior Gilbert smiling to see her there.

She sat down on the stool in front of his desk. There was a glass of red wine beside the book he was reading, noticing the direction of her gaze, he said:

'Would you take wine with me?'

There was a pause as she looked at the wine and Prior Gilbert and he laughed.

'Not I suppose very appropriate behaviour for a prior to drink wine in the middle of the night with a young maiden but I am old and beyond all measures of propriety.'

Without asking, he found another beaker and poured out the red wine which he handed to her.

'*In vino veritas*, you have come to discuss matters of great concern to you and also, to me, perhaps the wine will ease the flow of our conversation.'

She looked at the beaker without drinking.

'Have you taken wine before Isolde?'

She shook her head.

'How old are you now?'

'17.'

'Well, I think this is a good time to begin, wine you will know was the cause of the very first miracle at Canaan and it is on the subject of miracles that I think you have come to discuss.'

She admired the colour of the red wine and then took a careful sip; the liquid had a warm, deep taste which she wasn't sure she liked.

Prior Gilbert sighed, took a drink of his wine and tapped the desk in front of him with his fore finger, behaviour Isolde remembered, a sign which showed he needed time to think through the particular problem he was dealing with.

'To begin at the very beginning, when you came here after being saved from the sea, I asked you here in this room with Brother Gregory present, to say exactly what had happened. I was searching to see, you understand, whether this extraordinary salvation represented a miracle.'

She was watching him carefully, forgetting to drink the wine.

'And although everything suggested divine intervention for how could a small, weak child, survive the savage forces of the incoming tide in the dark of a winter night, there were no witnesses to provide the evidence required to make this a miracle.'

'But people at Lowyk, my friends, all those around me felt I had been saved, that there was a miracle, treated me as special, afterwards I had no friends, people would tease me, I never had any friends. What happened made me different!'

She almost shouted this out, her anger and distress palpable, then picked up her wine and drank.

Prior Gilbert nodded.

'There was little we could do, people knew the story.'

'You could have announced there was no miracle, that it had been a survival that had not involved the hand of God.'

'Is that what it was Isolde?' He looked at her carefully.

'I don't know, it was all such a long time ago.'

'But this is something you would remember.'

'There was this feeling of sudden calm, of being protected but there were no voices telling me what to do.' Her voice wavered.

Prior Gilbert remembering she was still unwell felt it wise to move on. He filled their glasses.

'You like the wine?'

She nodded.

'You asked me as I was writing the report whether I would teach you to read and write.'

Isolde leant forward now placing her elbows on the desk in front of her, waiting for Prior Gilbert to continue.

'I was going to refuse the request because this is a monastery and yes, a place of learning but not for girls. Then, you will perhaps understand, that I changed my mind because you had been saved, if there had been a miracle then there would have to be a purpose for this that you had, perhaps been chosen for a particular task.'

He continued, 'And that for this reason it might be important for you to receive an education here, be able to read and write because this might be something you needed in the future.'

Neither of them spoke, there was the sound of a strong wind both looked across to the window and the dark night outside.

'So, we arrive at more recent events.'

'Yes.'

'Do you want to tell me about it?'

There was no reply and Prior Gilbert remembered the very young girl finding difficulty describing what had happened.

Eventually, she spoke:

'So many dying, so much sorrow. Do you know what it's like hearing a small child calling out for their mother; frightened all alone, knowing they are going to die.'

She shook her head and then started to cry.

Prior Gilbert put a hand on her arm.

'You don't need to do this.'

But Isolde continued, speaking through her tears.

'This one girl brought in, three, four-year-old and the man who carried her shook his head to say...' Isolde looked up at him. 'She wasn't going to live.'

'He laid her down on the straw, just another small almost lifeless little bundle. Prior Gilbert, I was angry, why was this happening how could these small children be punished, they had done nothing, had had no time to be happy, they weren't ready to die, they needed life.'

'And so' – she looked down at her hands just as her smaller self had done all those years ago – 'I decided I would try and save her, took the cold almost lifeless hands and held them and prayed.'

She looked at him across the desk, challenging him to criticise, to say this was something she shouldn't have done, that she didn't have the right, the gift or the power to do so, but Prior Gilbert didn't comment, looking at her closely, waiting for her to continue.

She was crying again. 'Prior Gilbert, I have never prayed that way before, with all my strength I fought for the life of the child. My anger seemed to give me this special power, a kind of energy never felt before; I could feel some of my strength leaving me, transferring to the child.' And after a pause 'But perhaps this is just something I imagined.'

I spent the night with her and must have fallen asleep and when I woke I saw the sunlight across the floor of the chapel, the candle still burning on the altar and realised there was no one lying on the straw, just the shape where she had been lying, the child had gone, I thought she had died and been taken away.

Isolde wiped the tears from her eyes with the back of her hand.

'But she hadn't, the girl lived.'

'Yes, nobody could understand.'

'And they said it was a miracle.'

Isolde watched as Prior Gilbert, rose from his seat and paced across the room as he spoke.

'None of this is easy, Isolde, for you was it a miracle?'

He turned to her and in an almost menacing tone demanded:

'Did you bring the child back from what everyone says was almost certain death?'

He came and sat down back in his chair again, waiting for her response.

'I don't want it to be a miracle, don't want to be considered someone special and if I had the power to heal why couldn't I save other dying children?'

'Let's say for a moment this was a miracle, this time it was witnessed, poor Brother Andrew, May his soul rest in peace, who saw what happened for himself, felt something very special had taken place and that you had done this special thing.'

She shook her head denying what had taken place.

'It is worth considering a moment what a miracle represents. We live in a finite world which begins with our birth and ends with our death but we also believe that this is not the end that there is the infinite world of heaven a paradise that makes all our time here on earth worthwhile.'

He sighed. 'The question is how can miracles happen. The sick pilgrim who arrives at the shrine of a saint, here on Holy Island, at the relic of the Blessed Saint Cuthbert, how can this happen? I think the separation between finite and infinite can on occasion be broken, the person is healed through the intervention of the infinite world of heaven, through the mediation of the saint.'

'But there is this problem Prior Gilbert with the expectation that those who have made something special happen...' – he noticed how she avoided the word miracle – '...will be able to use their powers to cure further persons.'

'And there is then the anger of those whose children die and whom you are unable to save.'

'Yes.' And Isolde saw again the angry mother shouting at her because she had been unable to save her son, the face that returned in her nightmares.

'Our Sovereign Lord Jesus Christ did not save everyone; there were only a few miracles.'

Isolde stood up.

'Prior Gilbert, I don't want to be a special person, I want to lead a normal life, want to be able to go back to Lowyk and be accepted as just someone who lives there, not...not someone with the power to heal, to make miracles happen.

I am better now, it's time I returned to Lowyk.'

She got up and walked to the door, then stopped and turned to him.

'Did you arrange for Alan de Hetton to come?'

Prior Gilbert nodded.

'Thank you.' And then smiling and nodding as though reflecting on the new experience. 'I like the red wine.'

'Isolde, I need to inform you of a further matter which saddens me much. You will know that I have been prior here at Holy Island for many years and it is now time for me to hand over this position. Brother William of whom you are aware will take over as prior. I need to warn you about this man who has no concern for the wellbeing of those around him but is determined that the monastery here shall continue at whatever cost in terms of hardship associated with the payment of tithes. He does not also approve of women and has expressed concern that you have been allowed formerly to be educated here at the monastery.'

'Where will you go, Prior Gilbert?'

'I will retire to the village of Ellingham from where I come.'

'Well, then I will come and visit you there, as a friend.'

Isolde left, closing the door behind her and leaving the prior on his own and already, there was an absence in his life.

Chapter Seventeen

Isolde was not sure how she would be received on returning to Lowyk , not certain what she would find when she came back there. She came up with the cart of provisions from the monastery, although the pestilence had ended, there was little food to be found in the village.

She was sitting next to the carter a man of few words and the slow progression of the horse pulling the cart up the hill to the village gave her time to notice this place she lived, had spent her life, as though for the first time. People pointed her out, she heard her name.

The village was the same: the chapel, the small, mean, thatched cottages, little more than single-roomed huts, seeing them again now, spoke to Isolde of hardship and poverty. The ravages of the affliction however, meant the community seemed empty, many dwellings shut up where those who had lived there had died. There were fewer people walking around and their reactions strangely muted, moving slowly about whatever business they had now. The pestilence had delivered a terrible blow, recovery would be a long, slow process, the way of life of the community would need to change, nothing could be the same again. Over everything there remained the shadow of recent death.

As they arrived at her cottage by the chapel, Marjorie was there to meet her. She had lost weight and looked tired but the warmth of her greeting as she hugged Isolde was what she needed most on this return.

Gilbert Duff, headman of the village, a tall serious figure was organising the unloading of the cart and came across to her.

'Isolde, we are very pleased to see you here again, safe and sound. I want to thank you for all the work you did in the hostel.' He looked around at the other men carrying away the provisions for distribution and there was murmured agreement.

'It has been a terrible time and I don't know how we could have managed without you and Marjorie here and poor Brother Andrew's help. Lowyk will not forget your work with the sick and dying children.'

He paused here and frowned and she could see he was struggling to know whether to mention the saving of the dying girl. Then deciding this was not something to mention, knowing people's reaction had led to her sickness, he put a hand on her shoulder and smiled before moving away, giving further instructions to the men.

Soon after Isolde's return, there was a knock on the door and a girl of about her age standing there with a smaller child.

'You remember Sarah, Isolde, she wanted to come and say thank you.'

It took a moment for Isolde to realise who this was. She bent down as the little girl came and hugged her without speaking. Isolde held the small body a moment feeling the life there, hearing the breathing.

When she straightened up again, Isolde found she was smiling, couldn't stop smiling. A life saved to be lived, she thought, one small person's recovery from the pestilence and perhaps she had had some small part in this.

There was an awkward silence as no one knew what to say next but all three smiling, infected now by this sudden outbreak of good feeling.

The older girl spoke, 'My name is Angela, I'm her sister, her mother died and I'm looking after Sarah, she's such a good girl.'

'Does she remember anything?'

'No, just says you talked to her made her feel better, then she fell asleep and when she woke she was well.'

A meeting had been called by Gilbert Duff for the whole village of Lowyk to discuss the actions that should be taken now the pestilence had – perhaps only for the moment – left them.

They gathered for the big meeting in the space outside the church, used for these occasions. Men, women and children assembled; it took time for everyone to be in place ready to hear the announcements the headman would make.

'Friends of…'

Then he paused as the familiar figure of old John came limping through the crowd pushing his way to take his place at the front, making them laugh as they move aside to let him through.

'You still here, old John, thought you'd gone the journey.'

'Aye, happens I was oldest in village before pestilence, so stands to reason I'm oldest still now.'

Gilbert waited while someone fetched him a stool before starting again.

'This big meeting.'

Someone shouts out, 'Not many here Duffy for a big meeting, they al' deed!'

And another, quick as a flash, responds: 'Would be fewer if you hadn't been putting yourself about with the maidens, Robert man!'

There is an immediate outburst of raucous laughter from the men, which after a slight pause infects the women and then children, who without understanding didn't want to be left out of this reaction.

For the first time in months, here is something to laugh about and they gave in to a paroxysm of hilarity, slapping backs and turning with tears in their eyes to repeat the jibe while, the fornicator Robert stood looking embarrassed and his wife stormed away back to her dwelling, making it all the more funny.

Gilbert Duff raises his hand to end the commotion but it takes longer before they finally settle. A lad at the front of the crowd lets out a final false guffaw for which he receives a cuff around the head.

The headman is smiling himself now as he begins again with the arrangements needing to be made.

The list of actions to be taken is a long one. The huts of those who have died need to be burnt down to destroy any lingering infection, often with the bodies of those who have died still in place there. The hostel will be cleansed and those orphans who have no family and have no relatives to care for them, will be looked after by Marjorie and Isolde.

Then there is the matter of cultivation, with so many dying family strips will have been abandoned and those with adjacent areas are encouraged to take on some of this new farming commitment. Older children whose parents have died will help working on these new strips of land.

Gilbert Duff then turned to a matter of key importance to them, the payment of tithes to the Holy Island Monastery.

He looked at the crowd gathered in front of him.

'I learn from Isolde that Prior Gilbert, a good man who has been a friend to this village is to leave the monastery on Holy Island. His position as prior will be taken by Brother William from Durham who you will all remember from the words he spoke at the act of penitence in the priory church. Prior William will want to ensure the survival of the monastery and will consider the payment of tithes by Lowyk and each of the four other chapels essential.'

He now raised his voice, making clear his anger at this church imposition.

'We have suffered the loss of large numbers of our community perhaps almost half of those living here. For the next few years, it will be impossible for us to pay the tithes we will be unable to grow enough corn and beans. Much of the land will lie fallow, with no one to cultivate it, the production of food for the village and to feed the animals will therefore be severely affected. Even with the reduced population, it will be difficult to feed our own population.

What we will do therefore is bury the corn and beans into pits dug in the ground where they will be available when required by our own people and not be forfeited as tithes to the monastery on Holy Island. A place which has hardly suffered the affliction of the pestilence and has throughout the period had their larders full.

It will also mean that in the likely occurrence of further Scotch raids from across the border, these provisions will be unavailable to our enemies being hidden from view, buried in the ground.

A show of hands showed acceptance of this measure.'

Isolde's life in the village has changed; she has the orphans to care for in the hostel some ten small children for whom no homes can be found. They need to be fed and looked after, the community providing with the help of the monastery, the necessary food.

She finds there is a change in people's attitude to her. No longer someone different, who disappears across the sands to the monastery each week, she is now accepted, part of the community greeted with friendly comments as she meets people in the street.

It is also, now that Isolde becomes aware of her own beauty, as she moves away from giving a morning greeting to the women she overhears comments about her: 'Such a bonnie lass, "She is going to break hearts". And is aware men are watching her as she walks past, enjoying this new element in her life.'

Angela becomes a friend and they spend time together with the few other girls of their age and it is from her that she first hears about the May Day event on Dancing Green Hill, how this is something she must come to.

The occasion is shrouded in mystery, a secret event that has not been practiced in recent years that the girls talk about in lowered voices. There is a good deal of speculation about exactly what takes place. They have heard however that it is to be revived this year, unknown persons making the necessary arrangements. This is a celebration not of the blessing or harvesting of the crops, fixed events in the Christian calendar but rather something far older, a pagan rite to recognise the planting of the seeds, the flowering of the countryside, associated with the first of May; a rite which the church has successfully managed to ban, unhappy about the dancing and rumoured wild behaviour. People feel now, however, after the horrors of the pestilence, the need for its return, an act of liberation, a celebration of the ending of affliction.

The leading of a good life promoted by the church in order to achieve the salvation of paradise, is a doctrine that no longer has the same credibility, for why have so many children and good, innocent people died. The attraction of a gathering of young people to create pleasure is seen as a celebration of now, not the distant promised pleasures of paradise but something in the immediate. And there comes with the May Day event, the excitement of something forbidden, the appeal for Isolde of freeing herself from the clutches of the church and the burden of being different, a person with special powers, the chance, even for the limited duration of the rite, to break free from a lifetime of smothering goodness.

Leaving a meeting with Angela and their friends she stops to ask herself if this is really what she wants but is aware that the experiences she has been through have changed her and that she is ready now to embrace a new life, whatever that should bring. The spring rite will be the recognition of this new phase in her life, the bid for freedom.

Marjorie, surprises her by asking whether she will attend the ceremony on Dancing Green Hill. Marjorie has been at the event in some previous, distant year and while refusing to provide information on what actually happens, she prepares her stepdaughter. There is a plain white dress to wear, made specially, spring flowers to be picked to decorate her hair and then, on the afternoon of the event the preparation of the ointments, the juice of red berries for the lips, charcoal shading and underlining of the eyes and the application of scent around the neck and arms.

Then the golden hair is washed and brushed and scented, the primroses fixed there. Marjorie takes a step back to look at her girl. Doesn't say anything but nods in satisfaction at the beauty she sees before her. She holds her a long moment and then says:

'Dance away the night, Isolde, bring in the summer sun.'

There are tears in her eyes.

A horse and cart, parked a little way out of the village, will take the girls to Dancing Green Hill. Although a secret event many watch as the girls, 12 of them all in white dresses with flowers in their hair, make their way to the collection point. Isolde thinks as she joins them. "Like brides adorned for their husbands", only they are looking for another kind of experience, not one associated with husbands.

It takes half an hour to reach their destination and there is excited chatter on the journey, an infectious sense of anticipation as they head for an event they know nothing about. A flagon of mead passes around the cart. 'To give you courage,' says the girl next to her and Angela sitting on the other side laughs. The mead makes her feel light-headed.

The crags of Dancing Green Hill loom above them as they arrive and climb down from the cart. It is a perfect evening with not a cloud in the sky. Other maidens in white dresses, coming from every village in the district, join them, climbing up the path towards the crags. They can now hear the soft sound of a drum and pipe coming from the hill above them.

Isolde asks Angela as they walk up the path:

'Isn't something missing?'

'The lads I think they come up the other side of the hill.'

Some hundred girls gather on the summit flitting about like white butterflies, nervous about the approaching ceremony. They talk quietly, looking across at the boys now visible down the slope at the end of the green, the persons with whom, in some manner not entirely clear, they will soon be relating. Fresh flagons of mead are passed around.

The sound of a horn announces the arrival of the official party, the organisers of the event. A quiet and unexpected stillness descends over the green as the group, mostly older women dressed in special robes walk past them down the grassy slope, assembling just above from where the boys are now standing, tables and seats have been arranged here.

A younger woman has stayed with the girls to instruct them. Isolde notices, she is particularly beautiful, dressed in a more elaborate white dress with special necklace and bracelet, a snake tattooed on her arm. She is holding a staff decorated with animals and now speaks to them:

'You are participants in an ancient ceremony; this has to be done in a certain way. We will walk down the grassy slope, stop just above where our leaders are positioned. No, don't look at me, look straight ahead but listen carefully. As you walk, you keep your positions, do not speak, do not smile, look serious.'

'Now, form a line and join hands.'

The girls take their places, Isolde doesn't know the two girls next to her or where Angela has gone.

'When you stop, stand completely still, looking straight ahead, you do not look at the boys, fix your eyes on a position just above their heads. Is that understood?'

Nobody dares speak, awed by the strangeness of the occasion the elaborate ritual they have to follow.

'Advance!'

The girls walk slowly forward following the woman who holds her staff in the air. Isolde feels intense excitement, can feel the hand of the girl on her right shaking, turns to her to whisper:

'Have you ever?'

The girl who must be only fifteen looks puzzled a moment then understands and shakes her head.

The hills beside them are huge in the evening light, looking down on this ancient ceremony as the girls walk slowly across the grass, before coming to a halt, waiting in silence as instructed, trying not to look at the row of lads in front of them drawn up as though for battle.

From the corner of her eye, Isolde can see an older woman wearing a gown stand up from the throne she has been sitting on, a throne decorated with antlers. She speaks slowly and with solemnity, giving her words special significance.

'Welcome to this ceremony to greet the return of the sun, the time of fertilisation, when the seed is planted and there is the coupling of man and beasts.'

A shiver of excitement runs up Isolde's body as she hears these words, realising the vague rumours she has heard about this event are true.

'Since the beginning of time, there has been this celebration of May Day and as you dance through the night until the dawn comes, you will be doing what our ancient ancestors have done.'

There is a pause, then as she continues, her voice wavers.

'After the recent time of death and terrible suffering, there has to be a new dawn, new births to replace those many who have died, you young people.' And here she looks at the row of girls and there is a faint smile, before turning to the boys. 'You have this task to complete, your duty is clear.'

The leader is helped to sit down and another voice calls out:

'Let the dance begin.'

The music from a number of drums and pipes now strikes up.

On instruction, the girls turn to their left and in single file walk back up the hill to their starting point where they join hands again and are given further swift instructions because now the pace of the ceremony is to quicken.

'You are to dance in a line, holding hands and when you get to the point you reached before, look directly at the boys, choose one person to fix with your gaze and then, drop your hands and stamp your feet.'

Down the grassy slope in a skipping motion, the girls dance as the music quickens, the line now weaving in and out like a skein of wild geese, as they twist showing to advantage the white dresses, the decorated hair, the careful preparations made for this evening to enhance their appeal, to demonstrate the full attributes of their youth and beauty which at this moment of their lives is a celebration of their most heightened attraction.

Now in front of the boys, they stop, drop hands and picking up the hem of their dresses, lift them above their knees, to stamp their feet, aware of the boys watching them fascinated, aware of the excitement they are generating. For Isolde, the stamping is unleashing from the earth beneath them, some ancient force, something wild and forbidden associated with this business of fertilisation and insemination, this coupling of man and beast.

They turn and at a quicker pace are back to their starting point, as the movement is repeated. Only this time, they come closer to the line of lads who now put out their arms to try and catch hold of them. The girls fixing their attention on a chosen boy, deciding which one they would want to go with for this, inevitably, is what is going to happen.

'Now, move back!'

They dance back in line, keeping the formation as instructed, away from the grasping hands, following the shouted instructions. They are teasing the boys, the pace quickens, increasing hugely the appetite for the union which will follow. Isolde feels herself carried away with the joy of dancing, the excitement of the event and the anticipation of embrace.

'Forward again now!'

They are moving steadily forward, the stamping continuing until they are practically touching the boys.

The boys respond by picking up this rhythm of stamping feet, making the ground tremble before a signal has them forming a line to dance beside the girls as they move together up the hill, then around the fire at the centre of Dancing Green Hill which now, as the shadows lengthen, has been lit.

At a certain moment, as though through some unseen and unspoken signal, the lines join girl to boy, boy to girl, hands linked, the single line forming into a dozen, weaving their way across the green covering every section of the ground, keeping pace with the now frenzied music, so that when this finally stops the dancers collapse in a heap together, with the first embraces of the night. So that by the light of the fire, as the hills fade and the first stars appear, the couples are scattered across Dancing Green Hill.

Isolde's partner she had noticed from the first permitted glance at the young men, seen the way he had positioned himself so that he was directly in front of her as the stamping took place. Tall and good looking, immediately attractive and now together, she felt the pleasure of his embrace as his hands move across her body and she responds in equal measure determined to free herself from all that had gone before. His hand is now above her knee, her hand inside his breeches when the music starts up again and the dance continues a reminder the ceremony demands that they dance till dawn, until the sun rises on the magic morning of the first of May.

Before she has time to realise what is happening a girl has appeared laughing and pulls the boy to his feet, he bends down to give Isolde a last passionate kiss before being forced away to dance. All around them couples in the first throws of pleasure are being separated, is this a way to build desire, to ensure successful coupling?

There is no time to reflect on this as another lad, this time someone she knows from Lowyk has pulled her to her feet and dances away with her, kissing her on the neck as he does so.

'Ah, Isolde, such beauty!'

She smiles and kisses him back with equal passion, not remembering his name, but thinking, this is all wonderful as they whirl around dancing before joining others in a circle and somehow losing contact.

It is then, that a large, young man, catches hold of her hand and leads her to dance, there is no conversation or sharing of names. She knows here there will be an outcome and so, as they see others disappear into the long grass at the edge of the green, concealed from the light of the bonfire, he says, nodding towards a couple just disappearing from sight.

'You want this?'

And she nods, replying fiercely, 'Yes, I want this.' And he pulls her to where they can see others in copulation and there is an urgency for them, to do this act now.

He pushes her down onto the grass as she lifts her dress and he falls on top of her, pleasuring her with a long burst of moaning energy. He then gets up, pulls down her dress and leaves her doing up his breeches. She lies there looking up at the stars realising that this was something which she has enjoyed; here is finally the antidote to death, a suitable reaction to the dying and suffering that had taken up so much of her recent life. This place, this dance this fornication is the liberation she is seeking.

A table of provisions has been set up with jugs of red wine, bread and cheese, chicken and pork and she helps herself to a large beaker of red wine, finding she is soon surrounded by a group of young men wanting to dance with her, reminded of the way she had watched a female white butterfly surrounded by males wanting to take her and the way the female had lifted her abdomen to signal that she was ready for further copulation.

Several of the young have discarded their clothes and are now dancing naked around the fire which seems an appropriate response to the occasion.

Angela, one of these girls now comes up to Isolde, ceasing the beaker from her hand and draining the red wine it contains. Isolde sees her wild look, the dishevelled hair, the state of heightened excitement brought on by this rite of spring when, for one night all normal convention and appropriate behaviour can be abandoned.

'Take off your dress, Isolde, join us.'

Another girl from Lowyk comes up, encouraging her to do so.

Isolde refills her beaker and drinks further of the red wine as the girls keep up their demand:

'Devest yourself of the white dress, like Eve, in the Garden of Eden.'

And they rotate themselves around in front of her, showing off their naked bodies and laughing at the outrage of it all, the whole frenzied pleasure of the evening.

She has decided she wouldn't and shakes her head but the next moment they hold her, pulling the dress up over her head and she is being led to join the naked dancers by the fire, one of whom she notices is the beautiful younger woman who has given them instructions.

She admires the woman's body, the way she wears her nakedness, as though this is the most natural thing, the necklace and bracelet, the snake tattoo giving added attraction to the bare flesh. The lady notices the way she is watching her, comes over and kisses her on the lips, moving her hands over Isolde's body, exploring her nudity a softer touch, Isolde thinks, than the men she has already been with. The young woman takes Isolde's hand and makes her do the same to her, shaping the contours of her body, making her think of the form of the hills around them, the almost human shapes of this curving landscape. They kiss and touch some more, the woman pressing Isolde's hand where she wants the pressure, until responding with a sharp intake of breath, before kissing her again and drifting away with a smile and wave of the hand, as a young man pulls her from them.

Isolde considers all of this a moment, realising her education is being extended and wondering how she will seek forgiveness for all these accumulated sins.

Isolde didn't remember everything that happened after this. There were certainly other men and also girls. She knew this because she had an arm around the bare waist of a girl as they stood to celebrate the morning, saluting the May Day, as the sun rose over the sparkling sea. Isolde could see Holy Island and the familiar monastery wondering for a moment what she was doing engaging in this pagan feast which went against everything the church had taught her. Then the image came to her of the dying Henry and she saw again the face of the small boy, the weak smile that brought his life to a close, reminding her why she needed to extricate herself from this time with something strong enough to banish memories of the pestilence through this aggressive immersion in pleasure. And she turned and pulled the girl down onto the grass with her, giving in again to desire, the intoxication of ecstasy.

A group of young men, who it seemed had exhausted their energies, sitting on the grass chatting and drinking wine, were watching the two of them, and she was surprised to find that it pleased her that they were providing this spectacle. As she fell asleep on the grass with the girl, she thought it must be the many beakers of red wine she'd drunk that must explain her behaviour.

Angela woke her to say she was leaving that Isolde needed to come if she wanted to go back on the cart but Isolde wanted to stay on. The girl beside taking hold of her hand to stop her leaving, this was all too good to miss.

Waking later, she found the girl and most of the others had now left Dancing Green Hill. She sat there wondering what had happened to her white dress and how she was going to get home.

Then, someone was standing over her and she looked up to see a tall distinguished looking man, well dressed, who she hadn't noticed before.

She looked up at him and to explain her nudity, the evidence for her present state of heightened sin, felt it useful to suggest how this might be addressed:

'I think I will have to get to a nunnery!'

Chapter Eighteen

'I am Sir Robert de Bolam, Isolde.'

She notices the white dress he has folded over his arm.

'Is that my garment?'

He smiles and looks at the empty green around them.

'I don't see any other maiden who might be requiring to be clothed, do you?'

He hands her the dress with an elegant gesture of his hand and slight bowing of his head. She is thinking this is a knight he speaks and behaves in a special way, has manners. Did he come to rescue her, how would he know she was here, how would he know her name?

'You know my name?'

He nodded. 'I am a friend of Sir Alan de Hetton and came to find you.'

She put on her dress trying to understand why he would do this, not sure though that this is the time to ask. He helps her up and they walk together from Dancing Green Hill along a track behind where the lads had been standing at the beginning of the ceremony.

'Where are we going?'

'I have my horse tied up close to here.'

They come to the horse, standing feeding contentedly. He lifts her up onto the back of the animal and they walk on, Sir Robert leading the horse by the bridle. She has no idea where they are going or what they are going to do but it doesn't seem to matter.

The path leads through a wood; dappled light, patches of sunlight and shade. Isolde, feeling befuddled from the wine and excesses of the night, closes her eyes, enjoying the contrast between this sunshine and shadow, the steady rhythm of the horse's movement. A knight has come to find her, rescue her from the debauchery of the rites of spring, isn't that what knights do, protect maidens from dragons and evil, although he was a little too late. She lets herself fall forward, placing her hands around the horse's neck, enjoying the smell of the animal and falling instantly asleep.

He must have lifted her off the horse without waking her, for as she opens her eyes now, she is lying on the grass, covered by his cloak, in a small clearing, where there is a pond with rushes. He is tending a fire, the smoke rising up into the still morning air. Isolde closes her eyes quickly when he looks up, pretending to be still asleep, wanting time to think through what is happening, where all this is likely to lead.

He comes and stands in front of her, so she opens her eyes again.

'You might like to bathe in the pond, the water is clean.'

She looks at him and the pond with rushes.

'I have savon.' He hands across a bar of the soap which she has heard about but never seen before.

She gets up, undresses again and walks slowly into the pond, which is cool and refreshing aware of him watching her, thinking about how there is this problem of her being fair and

156

attracting the attention of boys and men, a new situation to deal with.

She uses the "savon" likes the scent and the effect it has but wondering how she is going to get dry. As she comes out of the pond, he hands her a cloth to dry herself.

'Are you ready to break your fast, although I think you have not actually been fasting?'

Isolde smiles at him and sits up as he brings her a plate of eggs and bread which she now eats looking around her, admiring this place he has brought her, thinking this has been specially chosen for its attraction: the pond, the surrounding silver birch trees with the first of their fresh green leaves, birds calling, everything about this encounter has been prepared and the food, providing something to eat here.

'Sir Alan de Hetton told me about you, Isolde, when he heard I was looking for someone to look after my children, someone who could teach them. I came to Lowyk early this morning to talk to you but found you hadn't returned from the spring ritual. Would it be Marjorie, I met who told me you would be on Dancing Green Hill? I didn't expect to find you but there you were, alone and abandoned and unclothed. I saw your dress near where the bonfire had been.'

'You had arranged to meet me and bring me here, give me food why?'

'To persuade you, food in a pleasant place, perhaps a way to get to know me. You see my wife died during the pestilence and I need someone to live in my house and look after the children and because you are educated...'

And young and beautiful she thought.

'You are exactly the person I need.'

A mistress, she thinks, to teach the children and be in his bed. She looks at him carefully considering how it would be living with him, this older man and decides this is not something she will want to do. Realising too that his impression of her will have been coloured by what he has seen already: the naked girl lying on the grass, having engaged in the famously lewd activities associated with the ancient pagan rights of spring. She could not pretend the innocence of the shy maiden.

This perhaps explains why, as he comes and sits beside her now, offering her a goblet of red wine and putting his arm around her. She responds to his approach and lying in the clearing they come together, the slow practiced fornication of a knight with the experience and knowledge to please and give extended pleasure. And of course, this is still May Morning when such practice must still, she thinks, be acceptable.

He turns to her to acknowledge her engagement:

'I see, Isolde, that you have a special appetite for this.'

Chapter Nineteen

Coming out from the hostel each morning there is the sight of Isolde, leading the small orphans. They walk behind her, holding hands, going out to where the strips of cultivated land begin and where the smaller livestock of the village are kept: hens, geese, goats and rabbits in a series of enclosures.

The children in pairs go to carry out their tasks which they enjoy, the oldest feed the hens and collect the eggs, others stay with Isolde to feed the other animals and clean their cages.

On this particular morning, Isolde is feeling tired and dispirited beginning to find the task of looking after so many children too much, wondering if there isn't someone else who could help her. Marjorie looks after the orphans through the night and early morning, and then hands them over to Isolde, keeping the two babies with her through the day.

Once the animals have been fed, the eggs collected, there aren't many other activities for the children to do except for walking around the village and into the country but the children are little and not able to go on long walks. So, generally they walk to watch anything of interest happening around the village before coming back to the hostel for some lunch.

Isolde is thinking as she watches the children collect the corn and feed the animals that she hasn't heard from Sir Robert and is beginning to think that the promised visit to his castle to meet his children, may never happen. Feels guilty for wanting to meet up and spend a night with him but wants in her life an element of excitement something to break the daily routine of looking after the children, trying to find ways of keeping them occupied.

Suddenly, there is shouting and laughter, voices raised in excitement and the clucking of hens coming from the chicken enclosure.

'Wait here, don't move,' she instructs the children around her. 'I will be back in a moment.'

She hurries off to the chicken pen to find Edward and William, the two eldest boys, throwing eggs at one another, there's a pile of broken shells on the ground. They stop as they see her, dropping the eggs they are holding onto the ground where they smash in a mess of shell and yoke. They are watching her to see what she is going to do.

'What are you doing?'

There is no answer.

Her anger is instant; she grabs each boy in turn by the scruff of the neck and smacks their faces hard, shouting at them. This is the first time they have seen her lose her temper.

She bends down and picks up a broken shell to make the point.

'This is food, eggs are valuable, we don't have enough to eat and you are throwing them at each other, breaking them, destroying food!'

There is a brief moment of shocked silence before William starts to cry, not quiet weeping but a howl of desperation which is immediately copied by Edward. First one, then the other calls out in their distress for their mothers.

The other children come to see what is happening. Then, a group response, the crying spreads, as the smiles of the person who loved and cared and looked after them who now they will never see again.

Isolde doesn't know what to do, this hasn't happened before. The children are bawling, the noise they make leading those working in the fields to look up from their work to see what's going on. Then instinct takes over, she gathers the children together as you might a group of small puppies, to contain them, keep them together into one sobbing snivelling group, tears streaming down their grubby faces, noses running. She bends down, making them hold onto her, putting her arms around them, holding them tight. Making soothing sounds to comfort them in their distress, thinking of the terrible predicament of being small and alone with no family in a cruel, difficult world.

'There, there, it's alright, I was cross, I'm sorry. I'm here for you, will look after you.'

Slowly the crying subsides and with a few last sobs, they fall silent but they still hold on to her, not ready to let go of this security. Isolde has become their absent mummy.

She thinks, as she holds them, how she is doing something important. Marjorie says many of them have nightmares and cry out in their sleep, what has happened to them will not easily go away.

After a moment, she says:

'Let's sit down.' And she gets them to sit down with her on the grass, the smallest closest to her, so she can hold them still. She needs to keep them calm, to reassure them, to take their minds away from their loss. So, she begins to tell them a story, something she hasn't done before.

'Once, Alan and I…'

'Who's Alan?'

'He's my friend; we decided to climb the rocky outcrop on Holy Island.'

She doesn't know why she has chosen this story but they listen, wide eyed at the account, as she exaggerates the terrible dangers, forgetting their own misery in the dangers of the climb: the violent wind, the cold, the wild sea just beyond them, the danger of falling at any moment from the steep path and being badly hurt.

Isolde makes the story last as long as she can, tells them of the trouble they were in when they get back to the monastery and how Alan is beaten.

This impresses them and they look at one another in wonder.

Edward asks: 'Will you beat us, Isolde?'

She shakes her head, and then to keep this moment of concentrated attention, she confides in them.

'Once Alan pushed me into a cupboard at the monastery and locked the door and wouldn't let me out.'

There is a shocked reaction to this. Why would he want to do this?

And Edward wants to know whether Alan was beaten again.

'No.'

And there are muttered comments on how he should have been.

Someone asks, 'So isn't he punished?'

'Yes, he has to become my friend!'

She can hear the children behind her talk about this, as they walk slowly, back to the hostel. Isolde thinking how she has found a way to entertain them, considering other stories she could tell.

She sees the horse first, tied up outside the hostel and then Sir Robert standing with Marjorie who is not looking very pleased at this visit.

Isolde isn't sure she wants to go with Sir Robert but the knight now comes forward and kisses her hand as the children stand around in a circle watching.

Sir Robert is good with the children showing them his sword and his horse, lifting some of them up onto its back and taking them a little way down the street of Lowyk. Isolde decides she likes him, and she wants to go with him.

There is a brief conversation with Marjorie who tells her she doesn't think this is a good idea but reluctantly agrees to look after the children the next morning.

They ride out together down the main street of Lowick, Isolde riding side saddle behind him, holding onto the knight, enjoying this close presence.

A small voice calls out: 'Goodbye Sir Robert, goodbye Isolde.'

And the other children repeat this, waving small hands.

She is pleased to be leaving, while only a matter of a month or two, it seems a long time since she has been away from the village and the orphans.

As they ride out into the country, she asks:

'Are we going to stop on the way, it's such a beautiful day.'

He turns and smiles.

'I know of a special place in a wood, where there is a pond and rushes surrounded by trees.'

'We could swim.'

He nods as the horse moves steadily on taking them to this place of pleasure.

Chapter Twenty

They arrive at Sir Robert's house in the early evening after spending a second period beside the pond in the wood with similar food and beverage and further fornication. This time he bathes with her and there is an excitement about the coming together of their wet, naked bodies, the increased desire this contact creates. And she enjoys again the practiced way in which he pleasures her. This is the new Isolde free of the constraints of the church and the demand for chastity.

Isolde has no regrets or sense of shame, her behaviour seems natural, a normal response to the particular situation in which she finds herself.

Sir Robert lives in a fortified manor house, there are servants and all the furnishings which are absent from her own home. She is given a long grey dress to wear which used to belong to his departed wife. Isolde puts it on, turns around admiring the way the long sleeves float as though independent of the rest of the dress. This is what being a lady means she thinks, living in a manor house with servants to look after you, a pleasant, comfortable life. Perhaps living here as Sir Robert's mistress would not be a bad choice.

Isolde comes down from the bedroom he has given her, down the oak staircase to the main hall, not used to stairs and careful to lift the corner of the long dress to avoid tripping, laughing as she does so at this need to behave like a lady.

She realises there is a man sitting at the long table in the centre of the hall watching her and immediately straightens and tries to appear ladylike to impress the unknown visitor.

The person stands as Isolde comes to the table and she notices his stooped and rather battered appearance, a face heavily lined, there is the suggestion of a full life, and she imagines experience of conflict. The man bows his head slightly to acknowledge her presence but says nothing, before resuming his place at the table.

At that moment, Sir Robert enters in a state of evident anxiety.

'I'm afraid, I shall have to leave you, there is an incident with two of my men someone has been killed and I need to deal with this immediately.'

He moves to leave them but turns to add:

'The food is ready and will be served with flagons of good red wine. I am sorry but this has to be…' He doesn't finish the sentence before disappearing out of the hall and into the courtyard; there is the sound of a heavy door slamming.

Servants arrive with plates of chicken and venison and the promised flagon of wine.

The man waits for them to leave before indicating to Isolde that she should take some food, taking out his knife and cutting a slice of chicken for himself. She is aware of being watched as she takes some venison.

He chews the chicken thoughtfully, and then pours them both a goblet of wine handing across her goblet.

There is an extended silence, and Isolde is wondering who this person could be. Why had Sir Robert chosen him to come tonight, when she had expected to be alone with him.

Then, he looked up.

'You don't know who I am, do you?'

She shook her head.

'I am Sir Alan de Hetton, father of your friend Alan, I have heard all about you and Isolde, you are every bit as beautiful as I had been led to believe.'

Isolde found herself going red, not sure whether she was embarrassed by this comment on her beauty or the sudden revelation, feeling that somehow her presence here now, was a betrayal of a special friendship.

She stood up, overcome by a sense of bewilderment that she couldn't easily have described and in this state of confusion made to come towards him, to greet this knight, the father of her best friend in a suitable manner. Wondering whether this was a moment when a lady would curtsey, however as she considered which foot to put forward to achieve this move, she tripped over her robe and fell at his feet.

Sir Alan, so affected by this unexpected fall, was quite unable to do anything but roar with laughter. Sitting on the floor looking up at him, Isolde, appalled by her behaviour, becomes in turn infected by the same complaint, laughing, the tears running down her cheeks.

It took a moment for them to recover and to be settled back in their chairs. Sir Alan kissing her on both hands in an expression of affection that pleased her. He pulled up her chair, so she could be next to him.

'So Isolde, my friend, I want to get to know you, to hear all about you. You know as a boy Alan, my son wanted to marry you.'

Chapter Twenty-One

It was a bright, late September morning and after feeding the livestock with the children, Isolde led them in front of the cages to where they could watch the final sessions of the harvest.

There were now more children in the group, some young mothers brought their infants to join them each morning, to listen to the stories and take part in the activities.

The stories had become a central part of each day. Isolde invited older members of the community to talk about how things used to be. Old John had been one of them but this hadn't worked as he sat looking at the children, while the children looked back at him, afraid to ask him any questions, Old John not knowing what he should say and perhaps intimidated by the small persons looking up at him, had after a moment stood up and left the hostel muttering something about "couldn't be bothered with young bairns".

It was as Isolde got the children seated in a line, which always took time that she noticed the riders, three of them among the harvesters.

She handed the biscuits baked by Marjorie that morning to Sarah to be distributed as she watched with growing concern what was happening on the fields in front of them.

Gilbert Duff must have been warned what was happening and he arrived now watching the scene; Isolde went to stand by him.

'They've been told where the pits are, someone's told 'em, bastard!'

And he pointed to the riders gathered at a particular spot where the main part of the corn tithe had been hidden. They dismounted and two of the men were lifting up the cover to the pit, carefully concealed with a turf lid. Harvesting had stopped as all now watched what was going on, gradually leaving their places of work to stand around where the riders were working.

'He'll have fled of course that John from Bowsden, I hope he has or he'll get his throat cut, that's for sure.'

Gilbert walked off to have conversation with the prior, joining the crowd who looked up as he arrived. Words drifted up to them across the field. She recognised the tall figure, pointing his finger at the reeve: William newly installed as prior at the monastery at Holy Island.

'Tithes payable to the monastery by law maliciously buried in pits, serious crime, severe punishment!'

Gilbert could be seen to gesture aggressively and now they were shouting at each other.

The children wanted to know what was happening, standing up to see better. They were worried about the shouting but it was difficult to explain. Susan who was now Isolde's helper talked to them quietly, trying to calm them.

Prior Gilbert could be seen to mount his horse and came riding over to them, followed by one other rider while the third man stayed by the uncovered pit to ensure no one tried to take the corn away.

The prior tethered his horse and came to where they were sitting, looking around him:

'Chickens, poultry, rabbits, small animals, they'll have buried the oats for them in a smaller pit somewhere around here, find it, Bernard!'

He looked up, noticed Isolde, and chose to ignore her.

The crowd of villagers now arrived and stood around trying to hinder the searching operation, this hiding place had apparently not been identified.

Prior William pushed people out of his way, an angry man, searching with darting glances for a patch of ground that looked different like a predator in search of its prey.

Isolde had noticed Mac was standing on the place where the corn was hidden he was a big man and moving him from there might be difficult, she thought, if he decided he wasn't going to move.

Prior William now turned to the children watching this spectacle, the most interesting thing they had seen on these morning excursions but they were also frightened.

'You boy there' – and he pointed to Edward – 'come here.'

Edward reluctantly got up and slowly walked over to where the prior was standing. He looked small and vulnerable as he stood next to the tall prior.

'You are going to tell me where the feed for the hens is kept.' A brief pause, then he raised his voice and shouted, 'Now!'

There was a murmur of discontent from the crowd of villagers gathered around the prior who now moved forward in a threatening manner as Edward turned to Isolde for help.

She was instantly on her feet, shouting at Prior William.

'You do not, Prior, at any time or for any reason shout out and frighten my children.' And pointing at the children, lowering her voice to underline their vulnerability. 'These are orphans, victims of the affliction of the great pestilence, they have already suffered enough, Edward, come here.'

Edward who was crying, nervous about being the centre of attention and being shouted at, ran back to Isolde who put her arms around him.

As the villagers looked in admiration at Isolde, Prior William surprised by this sudden outburst, became aware that the crowd was coming closer and that there was the danger of violence being committed on himself and his servant who had already been pushed over.

The man from the monastery decided at this point that it would be dangerous to remain any longer and so suddenly, pushed his way past the now menacing villagers and ran back to where his horse was tethered leaving his servant to extricate himself as best he could, receiving blows to his head and body as he did so.

A chorus of threats, oaths and laughter followed them, the children joining in, as the three riders hurriedly rode back to the safety of the Holy Island monastery.

Thus did the discovery of the buried tithes take place which would lead to terrible consequences for the village of Lowick in the year of our Lord 1353 in the reign of His Gracious Majesty King Edward, the Third of England.

End of Part One